In the light of the ritual ⟨W9-BYC-119⟩ —it was a tall shambling figure with blood on its head and unsteady feet. Next to it, wrapped in eerie robes, a woman stood. A low moan passed through her lips.

"A death rite," Professor Bergman said softly. "Such customs are common among primitives. They consider a sick man already dead and so they decorate his body with magical pow- ders to ensure his safe passage into the next world. Then they put him into a grave or on a pyre."

"Alive?" David said in disbelief.

The robed woman lit a torch and held it close to the face of the helpless man. As she was about to ignite his bed of sticks, Berg- man gasped, "David, that's Commander Koenig!"

COLLISION COURSE
was originally published by
Futura Publications Limited.

Books in the Space: 1999 Series

Breakaway
Moon Odyssey
The Space Guardians
Collision Course

Published by POCKET BOOKS

COLLISION COURSE

E. C. TUBB

PUBLISHED BY POCKET BOOKS NEW YORK

COLLISION COURSE

Futura Publications edition published 1975

POCKET BOOK edition published February, 1976

Standard Book Number: 671-80274-7.

Printed in the U.S.A.

To John, Alan, Steven and Lisa

COLLISION COURSE

CHAPTER ONE

Somewhere a woman was singing, her voice high and clear and achingly poignant. Koenig recognized the famous aria from *Madame Butterfly* and paused to listen, wondering if Puccini would ever have dared to imagine that he would have had his music played so far from home.

His music and the words which told so much. *One fine day . . .*

The day when they would all find a new home. When the runaway moon and base could be abandoned to continue the fantastic journey an accident had started. When the men and women comprising the personnel could settle down to rebuild their shattered lives. One day. One fine day.

Koenig hoped it would be soon.

Sighing he continued his progress down the corridor and into the Medical Centre. Helena was waiting beside a couch fitted with monitoring devices and he slowed a little, aware of her presence, her beauty. Hair, cut neatly in a golden helmet, aureoled her features which held a haunting slavic combination of prominent cheekbones, concave cheeks and a strongly determined jaw. Her lips were full, the lower sensuous, her eyes deep-set and oddly direct. The uniform with its white left sleeve enhanced the lush feminity of her figure.

Doctor Helena Russell, as Koenig had long since recognized, was a very remarkable woman.

'You're late, John.'

'I was distracted.'

'By the song?' Her voice was deeply musical. 'I heard it too. Cynthia has a beautiful voice but she should reserve it for more appropriate occasions. Now lie down on the couch, Commander. All the way, please.'

'Helena, this isn't necessary.'

'The mere fact that you say it isn't means that it is.' Her hands were firm on his shoulders. 'You're not a machine, John, so don't try to act like one. Too much depends on you for us to take chances. Regular checks may not be the full answer but they will help. Now just do what I say.'

It was hard to obey, to fall back on the couch, to attempt to relax as the woman fitted the monitors. Hard but it had to be done. Command-judgements should not be made by a man dulled with the toxins of fatigue, and there were mental as well as purely physical strains. Tension, maintained too long, becomes a habit, almost a way of life and to such a man reality is slightly altered to distort relative values.

Over three hundred men and women depended on Koenig for their very lives and he could never once dare to forget it. The black sleeve he wore signalled his authority, but the badge and symbol of rank did not make him a superman.

'Relax, John.' Helena glanced at the dials of the monitors. 'More. Take slow, deep breaths, think of something nice, roses for example. You like roses?'

'I used to grow them once. A long time ago now when I was studying on Earth. I had a box of soil and a few miniature hybrids and used to water them regularly each evening. The only trouble was that I could never keep the blooms. The other students used to raid the plants for gifts to give to their girls. Roses.' His voice thickened a little. 'Roses.'

'Perhaps you'll be able to grow them again soon.'

If so it wouldn't be on the moon, that he knew. They had no plants and even if they had the facilities were lacking. Soil and nutrients could not be spared from the essential task of food production to provide aesthetic pleasure. The hydroponic tanks, the yeast vats and algae cultures nurtured in the caverns dug deep below the base, warmed and illuminated by atomic power, demanded too much attention, too many precious man-hours of labour.

Another worry to add to the rest.

'You're still over-tense, John,' said Helena quietly. 'I'll have to adjust your blood-sugar content and equalize the endocrine balance. Of course the best thing would be for me to give you at least fifty hours Russian sleep.'

It was a temptation—fifty hours of oblivion born of micro-currents applied to the sleep centre of his brain. Instant repose during which his body, relieved of all mental strain, could heal itself.

'John?'

Koenig realized the hint had been in the nature of a question. And where, really, would be the harm? No one, not even he, was indispensable, the others could manage without him, Victor could

11

take over command. Fifty hours of induced sleep and he would be as good as new.

'John?' Helena was pressing. 'It won't take long to assemble the equipment and I could complete the monitoring while you rested. Yes?'

'No.'

She sighed, but had guessed what the answer would be before the question had been asked. Checking the instruments she glanced at his face, the eyes closed now as he tried to relax, some of the deepening lines smoothing from cheeks and forehead. He had grown older since they had first met, not in chronological terms, but in other ways. Responsibility had helped, but the greatest burden had been concern. The need to care for others, those over whom he was in command, those who depended on him for their continued existence.

The welfare of a world, she thought bleakly. John Koenig holds in his palm the welfare of an entire world.

The moon which had been torn from its age-old orbit about Earth, to be thrown into the uncharted depths of interstellar space, to experience the impact of alien laws of incredible sciences. As yet they had managed to survive but each day brought a new chance of unguessed peril and, always, was the fear that all their efforts to date could be washed out in a moment.

A blind man placed in a strange environment filled with spined and hooked objects, things edged and pointed and serrated with cruel indentations which could cut and tear and hurt at the slightest misstep. Or no, not a blind man, but a man born blind and suddenly given the gift of sight so that all he saw, all the colours he sensed, the shapes now grown abruptly unfamiliar, all would threaten his safety.

As the safety of the Alphans was threatened in this new and terrible universe.

The Alphans, the men and women who had staffed the base and who had lost their native world.

'Helena?' Koenig had opened his eyes and was staring at her with sympathetic concern. 'You're thinking, remembering.'

'Yes, John.' She was honest. 'Remembering—and hoping a little.'

Their hands met, gripped in a warm intimacy which required no words, the touch alone being enough. One day . . . one fine day. . . .

The hum of the commlock at his belt broke the train of thought. It was Bergman and his face was anxious on the tiny screen.

'Commander?'

'What is it, Victor?'

'Trouble. The sensors have spotted something massive heading directly towards us. John—'

Koenig snapped curtly, 'I'm on my way!'

Space was big but it was not empty. Stars, worlds, the fuzz of nebulae, the pale pulse of scattered galaxies all rested and moved in the overlapping energy fields of the universe. Dust gathered in opaque clouds in which suns burned like dying embers. Cinders drifted and enigmatic vortices gaped like monstrous traps to engulf anything, material or not, into their maws, to change it, to hurl it for incredible distances.

And there were scraps of debris, the broken fragments of disrupted worlds; pieces as small as a bullet, others like bricks, mountains, satellites.

The one heading towards Alpha was a jagged mass of rock thirty miles in diameter.

'There's no doubt, Commander.' Kano, at his post, ripped the print out from the computer and handed it over. 'It's all here, velocity relative to Alpha, direction, probable mass—from the figures it must have an extremely high mineral content.'

'Extrapolation?'

'Impact within thirty hours. Potential energy-release based on assumption of homogenous density stated in ergs is—'

'Save the science for Victor. Just tell me what the computer expects to happen.' Koenig was sharp and he knew it, but there was no time to be otherwise.

Kano pursed his lips then said, 'Two possibilities depending on exact mass of the approaching asteroid. One—the moon will be shattered into several fragments of varying size. Two—the moon will remain whole but a vast crater will be formed at the point of impact.'

'Which is?'

'Within fifty miles of the base.'

Kano's voice was flatly emotionless, but some things needed no emphasis. They were a target awaiting the impact of a celestial bullet. It would hit with massed tons of weight, potential kinetic energy which would be transformed into heat, itself and a chunk of the moon vanishing into converted radiation. Koenig had a vivid mental impression of a hammer striking a melon. If the hammer were light enough it would bury itself into the vegetable, heavier and it would smash it to pieces.

And the base was in the position of a fly sitting beneath the approaching hammer.

'Victor?'

Bergman drew in his breath, eyes narrowed as he studied the figures. Of all the personnel at their posts in Main Mission he was the least disturbed. Not because his mind could not recognize and appreciate the danger, but because his mechanical heart did not respond to the gush of adrenalin.

'Approximately thirty miles in diameter,' he said thoughtfully. 'That is about 3,400 cubic miles of rock. The probable weight based on the specific gravity of water would be . . .' He reached for a slide rule and shook his head as he noted the answer. 'High. Add velocity-mass to the total and we get—'

'Curtains,' said Morrow from where he sat at his console. 'Don't try to cover it up, Victor. 'We're all as good as dead and you know it.'

'We've been as good as dead before, Paul,' said Koenig sharply. 'But we didn't give up then and we're not going to give up now. We still have thirty hours and have a choice of action.'

'Such as?'

'Evacuation, diversion or destruction '

'Leave the target area, change the course of the asteroid or destroy it before it reaches us,' said Morrow. 'Commander! We can't leave! We've nowhere to go!'

'Which rules out the first possibility. Diversion, Victor?'

Bergman frowned, his heavy face sagging into deep creases. 'I don't know, John. It's barely possible but the time element is against us. By the time we get ready the asteroid will be too close and the amount of effective diversion too great.'

'Check with the computer, David.' Koenig waited

as Kano fed in the question and read the figures. 'Well?'

'The odds are against it, Commander, in the region of a thousand to one against success. That is allowing for optimum assembly of nuclear explosive charges.'

'Assembly and positioning,' said Bergman. 'We have no time to make certain that the mass of that asteroid is homogenous. If it isn't we'll shatter it into fragments and instead of diverting it we'll be on the receiving end of a shotgun blast.'

A rain of fragments any one of which would be enough to turn the base into molten slag. Even if they all missed the strains set up in the lunar soil would ruin the underground installations, smash the domes and turn the living and working quarters into wreckage. The end would be the same, complete and utter destruction.

'Which leaves us with no choice,' said Koenig grimly. 'We must volatize the asteroid.'

'Over three thousand cubic miles of rock,' said Morrow. 'And we have less than thirty hours in which to do it.'

'We'll do it.' Koenig forced himself to sound confident. 'Paul, instruct Carter to conduct a reconnaissance and determine the exact dimensions and material of the asteroid. Victor, get to work on the amount of nuclear explosives needed. Kano, search the computer files for all relevant information as to the placing of the charges, the probable results and the time-element of firing as applied to the optimum functioning of the base. Sandra, get me Anderson. Patch through to the communication post in my office.'

Behind closed doors, shielded from the eyes of

those in Main Mission, it was possible to relax for a moment, to drop the mask and let some of his anxiety show. A moment only, then as Anderson appeared on the screen Koenig was his usual self when faced with an emergency; a coldly determined man who demanded the impossible, confident that he would get it.

The chief engineer frowned as he heard the problem.

'We can adapt the Eagles, Commander, that's no real problem. External grapnels and interior releases—a dozen can be ready in as many hours. But the nuclear charges—that's something else.'

'Victor will take care of those. He's busy on the figures now, but I want you to start machining the casings and firing mechanisms straight away. We want fusion so we'll need a fission detonator incorporating remote control releases. Have them all synchronized to one master switch.'

'Safety factors?'

'One only. Have it fitted to the grapnel so the bomb will be primed and ready to blow as soon as it is in position.' Koenig shrugged at the other's expression. 'I know it's not what you'd like, but we have no choice. Time is against us. I want maximum crews and constant effort.'

'You'll get it, Commander,' promised Anderson. 'Anything else?'

'Yes—you can pray.'

Pray for a miracle to happen, for the threatening asteroid to vanish, to veer, to be swallowed up into the darkness from whence it had come. Pray that the charges and Eagles would be ready in time, that the figures would be correct, that the base would survive.

In Main Mission the tension was like a violin string tightened to breaking point.

'Eagle Eleven to Alpha. Nuclear charge in place. Mission complete. Returning to base.'

The voice of the pilot echoed his fear.

'Acknowledged.' Morrow turned in his chair and reported to Koenig where he stood with Bergman at his desk. 'Eagles Seven, Eight and Nine have returned to base, Commander. Eagles Ten, Eleven and Twelve have laid their charges and are returning.'

Koenig nodded as he looked down at the model on his desk. It was a replica of the asteroid constructed to scale, the surface marked with eleven pins each representing a nuclear bomb. In the main screens the actual asteroid could be seen, magnified, the rugged surface pitted and sere.

It was a relief to look up at the space windows, to see the shapes of the returning Eagles as they grew large in the empty void. An illusion, the Eagles were not growing but coming closer and the void was not empty, soon the bulk of the asteroid would dominate the heavens.

From his post at the computer Kano said, urgently, 'Commander, Eagle One is in trouble. The schedule has not been maintained.'

'Paul?'

'I'm making direct contact, Commander.' Morrow worked at his panel, grunted as Carter's face appeared on the screen. 'You should have placed that charge by now. You haven't—what's wrong?'

'Malfunction in the main booster, I think. I can't get the speed.'

Koenig moved forward to stand behind Morrow, looking over his head at the screen.

'Alan, we must detonate the nukes in two minutes. Can you make it?'

Carter was grim. 'I'll make it, Commander. All the way.'

If it could be done then he would do it, Koenig knew, but sometimes sheer determination and courage wasn't enough. An accident, a freak which had caused the malfunction, the unknown factor which was always present in the affairs of men.

One which could cost Carter his life.

'No,' said Bergman as, turning from the screen, Koenig met his eyes. 'We can't abort Carter's mission. That charge he's carrying has to be placed in order to ensure the total volatization of the asteroid. We're operating on a minimum as it is.'

As if to emphasize the situation Kano spoke quietly from his post.

'We're losing the time-line, Commander. Alan will need a minimum of a hundred and ten seconds to get clear of the asteroid before we detonate if he hopes to survive.'

The life on one man against that of hundreds, one Eagle against the entire base. The ship was nothing, but the man was not. He was a living, breathing creature, a comrade, a friend.

Koenig said flatly, 'Delay the blast forty seconds.'

'John we can't do it!' Bergman was adamant. 'We must destroy the asteroid to avoid collision. Timing is vital to prevent us from being caught in the radiation cloud. There will be plasma stretching in all directions and we will still be in the direct line.'

'I know that.'

'Then—?'

'Delay the blast forty seconds,' repeated Koenig.

'That is an order.' He turned again to the screen. 'Alan, don't waste time on perfection. Get in and get out fast.'

A gamble, but one he had had to take. A valuable life against a few seconds of time, but there had been a minute safety factor and Koenig felt justified at having used it.

He heard Morrow sigh as the Eagle landed, his startled curse as the charge it carried remained attached to the grapnel as it rose.

'Alan! The charge, man!'

'It's stuck!' Carter's voice was strained as it came from the speakers. 'The release mechanism's jammed.'

'It's got to be placed, Alan!' Morrow was sweating, sympathizing with the distant pilot, sharing his dilemma. To run and save his life or to stay and ensure the success of the operation. To run was to kill them all, but to sit, waiting, for the bomb to explode . . .

Bergman said, sharply, 'He's leaving.'

'No.' Koenig had recognized what was happening. 'He's trying to jolt it loose. See?'

On the screen the Eagle was performing a strange series of gyrations. Up, down, halt to rise again. Twice, three times—and then the bomb fell clear.

'She's gone!' yelled Carter. 'I'm on my way back!'

Too late, they had lost the time-line, but Koenig had to be certain.

'Compute!'

Kano said, evenly, 'Blast in ten seconds, nine, eight . . .'

'Delay ten!'

20

'Commander?'

'You heard me! Delay ten!' Precious seconds to give a man a chance to live. 'Paul, activate all radiation screens to maximum intensity. Red emergency alert. Seal for impact.'

Things which had already been done and Koenig realized that he was talking to avoid having to face the probable results of his impulsive decision. Seconds now, falling as they were counted.

'Five, four, three, two, one—zero!'

Space filled with a living, writhing gush of flame.

CHAPTER TWO

Flame expanded to spread and engulf the face of the moon, the base itself in a cloud of radiant particles. Matter had been transformed into energy by the synchronized detonation of the twelve nuclear devices, the main bulk of the asteroid turned into a plasmic, radioactive gas. But some fragments of solid material still remained and, like a rain of hail, scraps of debris gouged craters from the lunar plain, others flaring as they struck the protective shields of the base.

Tensely Koenig listened to the stream of reports which told of the result of his gamble. They had been fortunate, some minor cracks and distortions, a temporary loss of power to various parts of the installation, a roof collapsing in a lower cavern. A muscle jerked on his cheek as Medical Centre reported fourteen casualties.

'Check that, Paul. Radiation?'

'No, Commander,' said Morrow after a few moments. 'Only conventional injuries have been reported as yet.'

A cause for relief and yet it was early for symptoms to show. Later, when cells were dying and mutations had resulted in wild cancerous growths, there could be a different story. But, for now, first things had to come first.

'Have you made contact with Eagle One yet?'

'No. I've been transmitting on automatic but as yet there has been no response.'

'Keep trying. Maybe he can't transmit for some reason, but it may help him to know that we survived.' Koenig moved to stand beside Sandra Benes at her post. 'I want a total scan of the immediate surround. That Eagle is up there somewhere and we should be able to spot it.' He noticed her expression. 'Something wrong?'

'It's the plasma field, Commander. Nothing can get through it. We're enveloped in an electronic fog as well as being visually blind. Alan could be up there if his shields held and he wasn't destroyed, but we can't spot him.'

Not for the present at least and later might be far too late. Carter could be hurt, unconscious even, his ship drifting, carried on the blast of the explosion in which case he would be completely lost in the void by the time any of the base scanners could function.

'We'll have to go and look for him,' said Koenig. 'Once we're free of the plasma field it should be possible to establish contact. Paul, have an Eagle made ready. If Alan is out there I intend to find him.'

Bergman looked up from where he stood studying a flowing line of figures on an illuminated plate; the radiation counts and energy levels recorded by sensors set in and around the base, others situated far beyond the protective shield.

'I wouldn't advise it, John,' he said flatly. 'Can you guess what it's like out there?'

'Bad.'

'It's a radioactive nightmare. Even the instruments seem to have been affected by the release of unusual forces. My opinion is that you should wait until the electronic storm has diminished to tolerable levels.'

'We have shields,' reminded Koenig.

'Shields which may not be effective against the energies I have registered. The intensity is fantastic. The nuclear devices seem to have triggered off the very constituents of the asteroid itself so that, in effect, we created a miniature sun. The duration was fortunately brief but residual forces remain. Not only that but space is still filled with debris. Some of it is bombarding Alpha.'

'Without Alan it wouldn't be debris,' reminded Koenig. 'We'd have the shattered bulk of the asteroid in our laps. And we wouldn't be standing here arguing about it. We'd all be dead, Victor. Dead!'

'As Carter might be at this very moment, John. You gave him every chance you could, but the possibility of his managing to survive is very small. The initial blast—only a freak combination of circumstances could have saved him. Surely you must realize that.'

23

'Luck,' said Koenig quietly. 'Maybe we're getting used to it, Victor. Or maybe it's a simple thing called faith. But luck or faith makes no difference. I have to look for him. I have to know. Can you understand that?'

'Must you go yourself, John? Alan is a good friend, I know, but you are responsible for the base. Your first duty must be to the lives in your keeping.'

'It is. I can't order anyone to go out there and search for the Eagle. You're in command until I return. Paul, get that ship on the pad and ready to leave and see if you can find an idiot to come with me.'

'You've got him, Commander.' Morrow rose from his consol. 'I'm worried about Alan too.'

The explosion had been a hammer which had sent echoes from the hull, sounds to ring and reverberate in his skull, a tremendous force which had flung him hard against the restraints, which had drained the blood from his brain to throw him into a dark oblivion.

Alan Carter stirred, conscious of a blur of noise, a voice like the thrust of a stabbing knife.

'Wake! Wake and attend your vessel!'

Words in his mind, a ghost voice, disembodied, coming from no normal throat. Yet the words made sense. Light burned his eyes as he parted the lids to look at massed dials, warning flashes, dancing needles. Sound roared from the engines, a jarring thunder of uncontrolled power and slowly his hand lifted to fall on a lever.

To fall and press, the sound dying as the control responded.

Another voice, harsher, more urgent.

'Alan, answer. Do you read me. Koenig here. Answer if you hear me. Come in Eagle One. Eagle One answer . . .'

Too harsh and too urgent. Carter closed his eyes and sank back into a place of entrancing delight, a misty world in which nothing bad could possibly happen and, like a child, he wandered through brightening passages to where in a hall of enigmatic shapes a figure waited.

'Mother?' He was running. 'Is that you, Mother?'

'No.'

A flicker and he was no longer a child but a man, his outlook and mind changing as if a page had been turned in a book.

'Clarise? It's you, I know it is. Why did you leave me at the party and hide?' He looked at the strange room in which she sat, his eyes disturbed by lines and planes which refused to retain recognizable form. 'Clarise?'

'No.'

'Who then?'

'A friend. You may call me Arra.'

'Arra?' Carter frowned, thinking, trying to remember. 'I don't know you. We've never met before.'

'That is unimportant. Now you will come a little closer, that's right, more now, more. Sit and rest your hands . . . so. Lean back and place your head . . . so.'

It was a dream, it could be nothing else. The weird chamber, the enigmatic figure dressed all in black, the face veiled, the hands covered, the voice —what was so odd about the voice?

There was something imperious about it and yet

something sad. A musical resonance which held an indefinable yearning. The voice of an angel or of a woman lovely beyond imagination. The quintessence of feminity now sitting before him in a chamber composed of alien forms and indescribable colours.

A voice which sang and whispered in his mind, comforting, reassuring, soothing, commanding, ordering him to sit on a puff of vapour, to rest his hands on spindled shapes, to lean back and surely to fall. But he did not fall and the vapour became the familiar contours of a chair, the spindles the well-known array of controls, the winking eyes set about the mysterious chamber the dials of instruments.

And the voice had changed.

'Eagle One. Carter, answer if you can. Come in Eagle One. Give position and condition. Alan, this is Koenig. Paul is with me. We're looking for you. Activate location beacon at full intensity if you receive me.'

Koenig and Morrow? John and good old Paul coming to get him? But where was he and what was he doing? Carter looked blearily at the controls, the instruments. He was dreaming again. He must have fallen asleep in the mysterious chamber —no, that was a dream too, so he must be in bed at the base and all this was the product of a nightmare.

'Wake and take control!'

He jerked to the mental impact of the voice, no longer soothing, no longer kind. It held a savage ruthlessness, the snap of command. The tone of one accustomed to being obeyed.

A thought occurred to him, a scrap of memory

26

from the distant past. A road busy with a stream of cars. A group of children himself among them. A man giving a warning.

'You have the right to cross the road at this point and all traffic is supposed to stop for you. But remember this, you putting up your hand doesn't stop the car. The man inside does that. Sometimes he's too slow or he may not see you or the brakes may fail. So never make the mistake of thinking that because you give an order or a signal, that order or signal, by itself, does anything.'

One of the boys had forgotten and had later been killed.

I understand. Relax and do not resist in any form. Open your mind.'

The voice, again soothing, comforting, the tone of a mother who had recognized her impatience, the fact that she had asked too much.

Carter felt his hands move in a pattern learned and impressed on his brain over long and arduous years of training. He knew what to do—something or someone now gave him the strength to do it, was using his body as his mind sank blissfully into an ebon cloud.

'Paul!' Koenig's voice was sharp. 'The signal! Carter's activated the beacon!'

He sat hunched forward in his chair, the discomfort of his suit forgotten, the danger all around dismissed in the flush of potential success. For too long they had driven through the radioactive cloud, the shields at maximum intensity, the tell-tales edging higher and higher towards and into the red.

'Paul?'

'I'm getting a fix,' said Morrow. As Koenig took

over the controls the pilot busied himself with delicate verniers, judging time and distance, making allowances for external distortions, using skill and knowledge to augment a calculated guess. 'Bear fifteen degrees right, twenty-two up.'

Koenig's hands froze on the controls as he was about to follow the directions.

'No,' he said.

'Why not? The beacon—'

'What you're picking up is a reflection. If we chase it we'll lose the Eagle and Alan for certain.' He moved the controls, sending the Eagle through the plasmic cloud on a path at variance with the directions given by Morrow. We'll find Alan in this area, I'm sure of it.'

'How?'

'How, what?'

'How can you be sure, John? All the instruments say different. You're running blind and operating on hope. If we—' Morrow broke off, staring at a lamp which flashed on the panel. 'The responder! It's the other Eagle, Commander! We've found it!'

It looked like a thing long dead, the hull scarred, blistered, the bare metal seared despite the protection of the shields. If Carter was alive he gave no sign and, after the third attempt to make contact, Koenig gave up.

'We'll have to dock and arrange an exchange,' he decided. 'Take us close, Paul, and I'll couple the air-locks.'

'In this?' Morrow's gesture at the cloud outside was expressive. Tiny flashes of light, glowing winks of fire, a turmoil of cooling vapour, the whole laden with radioactivity as if it were an illuminated, lethal mist.

Within the ship the protective shields would save them, outside only the metal and fabric of the suits would stave off imminent death.

'Make contact, energize the magnetic grapnels and head towards the edge of the cloud,' decided Koenig. 'As soon as we're in the clear I'll make the exchange.'

Morrow was an excellent pilot, the jar as the two hulls touched was barely noticeable, and with deft touches of the controls he kept the vessels firmly joined as he guided them in a direct line which would carry them beyond the turmoil of the cloud.

As the swirling vapour began to thin, gases travelling at high velocities and cooling as they expanded to form a diffused scatter of minute debris, Koenig moved through the ship towards the airlock. Sealing the inner port he fastened himself to the bulkhead with clips attached to straps; a precaution, if the outer door had been damaged and should open too quickly, the expelled air from the vestibule would take him with it and hurl him into space.

'Paul?'

'When you're ready, Commander.' Morrow's voice came clearing over the helmet radio. 'Area relatively clear and I'm holding a steady velocity.'

'Commencing exchange procedure—now!'

Koenig hit a button, watched as a light flashed from green to yellow, saw the movement of an instrument as air gushed from the small compartment into space. As the light changed to red motors disengaged the locking doors and the outer door swung open.

Unclipping the restraints Koenig stepped to the edge of the portal.

Before him the other Eagle filled the sky, apparently motionless as it rode beside his own vessel. The air-locks were not aligned closely enough for a communication tube to be established, but that was unimportant. A kick and Koenig had crossed the gap, gloved hands catching at the portholds. The external control was set beneath a plate held by a simple catch. Heat had fused the metal and he grunted as he slammed the heel of his palm against the control.

'Trouble, Commander?' Morrow had heard his breathing over the radio, his muttered curse. 'Need help?'

'No. The catch is jammed, but I can free it.' A final blow and it yielded. 'I'm about to go inside.'

Seconds dragged as the outer door closed and air gushed from within the ship to replace the vacuum. As the pressures equalized the lamp flashed green and, impatiently, Koenig thrust open the inner door.

At first he thought Carter was dead.

The pilot was lying back in his chair, his face pale and strained beneath the visor of his helmet, a thin trickle of blood showing at the corner of his mouth. Koenig checked the pressure, found it acceptable and freed the pilot's helmet from his suit. A geiger counter fastened to the wrist of his suit registered high, but Koenig wasn't interested in the duration of his exposure to radiation. Holding the polished metal to Carter's lips he sighed with relief as it misted.

'Commander?'

'He's alive, Paul. Unconscious, but alive.'

'Thank God for that! Hurt?'

'I can't tell. No sign of external injuries but there could be internal damage. When the charges blew he must have been subjected to a tremendous shock.' Koenig looked at the controls and instruments. 'The panel's in a mess too. We'll have to go in together. I'll stay here and do what I can.' He frowned as Morrow made no reply. 'Paul?'

'I don't believe it,' whispered the pilot. 'I simply don't believe it!'

'Paul! What's happening? Report!'

'The screens! Look at the screens!'

They were inoperable, the surfaces remaining black as Koenig hit the switches. Turning he ran back into the air-lock, sealed the inner port, waited, fuming as the cycle was completed and he could step into space.

Once opened, he surged across the space, back into the other vessel, to stand in the command module and stare at what Morrow had seen on his screens.

A planet where no planet should have been.

A tremendous world against which the bulk of of the moon showed like a pea set before an orange.

A wall in space against which they would surely crash.

CHAPTER THREE

There was time, there was always time; time to ponder the impossible, to pray, to question, to defy the fates and deities which threatened their survival.

A game, thought Koenig bitterly. We are pawns torn from our own place and time by a cosmic upheaval, sent to wander like nomads in an unfamiliar cosmos, drifting between the camp-fires of alien suns, contacting worlds on which we cannot survive. It was inevitable that, eventually, they would meet one problem that couldn't be solved, one danger which they couldn't avoid.

But they were men and, because of that and their heritage which had lifted them from mud to the stars, they would fight to the last.

Fight with words, ideas, concepts and, when all else failed, with hope and faith.

And, always, with action.

'There is a mystery about this planet,' said Koenig. 'We had no reason to suspect its existence before we destroyed the asteroid. Certainly we didn't see it. Now, abruptly, it is here. A world thirty times the size of the moon.'

'Thirty-four, Commander,' corrected Kano. He sat with the rest of them at the desk in Koenig's office. 'The computer holds no data as to its origin.'

'Which means that it appeared from nothing,' said Morrow. 'Which is just what it did do. I was watching. One second space was empty, the next that thing was hanging in the sky. Victor, could it be an illusion?'

'No.' Bergman shook his head. 'It is tempting to think so, that it is a form of spacial mirage which has been formed by some freak of diffused radiation and dimensional warping, but our sensors report the presence of mass.'

'Density?'

'Extremely low, John, but high enough to utterly destroy us should we collide with it. The problem is similar to the one we recently faced with the asteroid. Unfortunately we cannot use the same solution. We don't have enough nuclear explosives to destroy a world even if we had the moral right to do so.'

Morrow said, grimly, 'This is a matter of survival, Professor. What have morals to do with it?'

'There could be people on that world, men and women and children, living, thinking and feeling beings who have the right to be considered. Are you willing to destroy them all?'

'It isn't my choice,' snapped Morrow. 'If we hit them they will die anyway. We will all die. I'd rather it be them, if they exist, than us. Sorry if my ideas offend you, but that's the way I'm made.'

'Life at any price,' said Bergman slowly. 'But sometimes the price can be too high.'

The mechanical heart he had been given and which had enabled him to live when the woman he had intended to marry had died. The price he had paid for a life in which he was divorced from all extremes of emotion so that, to strangers, he appeared to be a living machine made of flesh and blood and bone.

Koenig said, abruptly, 'We're wasting time. We have little more than a hundred hours before we strike and we have still to formulate a plan. Paul?'

'I say we try to divert our path. We could repeat the original blast which threw us off orbit. In a minor degree, naturally, but it should work.'

'David?'

'Any such attempt would be fraught with the highest danger,' said Kano precisely. 'Old fissures which were then strained could easily yield under the impact of a second explosion. Also the degree of deviation required is too great to be achieved without using more explosives than we have.'

'Then let the moon split,' snapped Morrow. 'As long as the base remains intact what does it matter?'

A good point, but Koenig recognized the difficulties which the other had overlooked.

'We've no time to plot fissure-lines, Paul. And we have no way of assessing the degree of deviation obtained from any explosion. Victor?'

Bergman had been studying lists of figures; he looked up, frowning. 'John, I want the complete use of the computer for the next two hours. Also the records of all atomic experiments in the restricted file.' He smiled at Koenig's expression, remembering. 'Of course, we have no restricted file now, I'd forgotten.'

'You've an idea, Victor?'

'As yet a vague one, but it could provide the answer. When we destroyed the asteroid the instruments showed irrational findings, at least I thought they were irrational at the time, now I'm not so sure. There was an inexplicable energy-loss from the nexus of the plasma cloud. I'd made the most careful calculations as to the mass of the asteroid, the amount of nuclear explosives used and the anticipated extent of fusion achieved, but the figures didn't match.'

Bergman turned to Kano. 'Bad mathematics, perhaps, David, which is one of the things I want to check.'

'You can use the computer,' said Koenig. 'But just what do you hope to find, Victor?'

'A method by which we may save ourselves. Not by destroying either that planet or our moon, but by diverting them by a sub-etheric shock wave triggered by an atomic blast. These figures have given me the clue. If we detonate several opposed amounts of nuclear fuel at a precise distance we create a sub-atomic vortex which will act not on the actual particles of matter but on the sub-spacial matrix which confines them. We will move the mortar between the atomic bricks and, by so doing, move the bricks also. You see?'

'Of course,' said Morrow, dryly. 'It's simple. Why didn't we think of it before?'

He was being ironic, but the irony was an expression of relief as Koenig knew. A relief he shared. No matter how slim, they had a chance.

'Let me get this straight, Victor. You intend to explode a mass of nuclear material between us and the planet. Right?'

'Yes. The exact position has to be determined, of course on a basis of relative mass.'

'And you hope to create some kind of shock

wave which will force us apart or, at least, divert
our path so as to avoid collision. Yes?'

'John, I've explained all this. As yet the possibility of success is problematical and yet I am
certain that with the data so far obtained I can
achieve that result.' Bergman took a sip of water.
'Think of it as a match lighting a paper which lights
some wood which lights coal to melt ore to make
steel—the detonator series which works in a car-
tridge or a bomb or a nuclear device. One energy
level affecting another. What we need to do is to
reach a sub-spacial level which can be done by
using the very force of the blasts against each other
to form a warp which—'

'Please, Victor, no lectures. Save the figures for
the computer. But you'll need all the nuclear explosives available.' Koenig thumbed a button on
his desk and to the face which appeared on the
screen gave the necessary orders. 'All stocks,' he
ended. 'Strip the piles down to minimum require-
ments for the maintenance of the base.'

'Right, Commander. Time?'

'Fifty hours.'

Fifty hours. Half-way to the mysterious planet.
Half-way to death.

Doctor Bob Mathias paused on his way through
Medical Centre to check the monitoring instruments
attached to the figure lying on the couch. Carter
was still unconscious; nothing to worry about as yet,
but if the condition continued for another two
days stringent measures would have to be taken.
The facilities of the base were not enough to maintain anyone in a state of permanent coma.

Passing on he slowed as Helena came from the

diagnostic room. Behind her the shapes of enig-matic machines showed dimly beneath a glow of blue, ultra-violet-loaded light, tiny lamps winking like a host of colourful stars, meters ranked like staring, watching eyes.

'Any change, Helena?'

'In Carter's condition? No.'

'We could apply electrical stimulus direct to the cortex,' suggested Mathias. 'The reaction could snap him out of his disoriented condition.'

'You think that is what it is?'

'With complications, yes.' Mathias was definite. 'His sensory apparatus was subjected to tremendous strain both in the initial explosion and the radio-active plasmic cloud which followed. The shields saved him from immediate physical destruction, but his central nervous system was overloaded and his thalamus confused to the point where sanity could only be maintained by mental escape into uncon-sciousness.'

Helena nodded, thoughtful. 'You regard Carter's condition as an almost classic case of withdrawal syndrome?'

'To me it is obvious. A man, in peril of his life, mind and senses, confused, faced with either outright insanity or the shutting down of his mental receptors so as to hide in mental oblivion. Now he has to be wakened, as it were. Reassured as to his safety.' Pausing he added, grimly, 'You don't need me to tell you, Doctor, that the longer the condition is allowed to continue the harder it will be to overcome.'

'No,' said Helena. 'You don't have to tell me. But there is no point waking him to suffer avoidable physical discomfort.'

It was a minor conflict which she, as the higher ranking of the two, would win if disagreement over a patient's welfare could be considered a battle. Yet Mathias was right and she knew it. The mind, the all-important ego, was of far greater consequence than minor torments, but for reasons of which Mathias as yet knew nothing, she wanted to delay.

'You're right, Bob,' she said with abrupt surrender. 'I'll make a detailed check and then commence treatment to restore his awareness. I would be pleased if you would assist me in the later stages. Say fifteen minutes?'

Mathias nodded and moved away to tend to other patients as Helena crossed the room to Carter's side. He looked very pale, his muscles flaccid, the arm she lifted falling back without the slightest trace of resistance. His breathing was regular and shallow, his blood-sugar low, the quivering lines of his electrocardiogram showing a low level of metabolic activity.

It was to be expected—two days in a near-coma would have produced exactly that result, but the encephalographic pattern was not what she would have expected.

Frowning, she rechecked the monitors.

The brain, in essence, is a computer working on minute currents of electrical energy, the cells organic data banks, the connections threads of neuron tissue—the entire thing incredibly complex. Carter had been blasted with tremendous forces, bathed in wild radiations which, even though baffled by the shield, would still have left traces.

Helena turned a mercury switch and watched the stream of figures pass across a screen from the geiger counters monitoring the pilot's blood which

38

was being passed through a system of filters designed to 'wash' away any dangerous radioactivity.

They too were as she had expected. The level was safely low which meant the bone-marrow was uncontaminated and that the red and white corpuscles were in correct ratio.

Switches closed beneath her hands as she shut down a part of the monitoring panel; the prelude to commencing the waking technique. Other dials glowed into life as a pump whined to hyperoxygenate the filtered blood.

Something touched her hair.

For a moment she froze, stunned by the unexpected, feeling hands at the nape of her neck, fingers lifting the mane of her hair. Carter! Rearing up behind her, reaching, touching . . .

She spun and stepped back, seeing his face, his eyes, the terrible intensity stamped on his features.

'No! No, Arra! Don't leave me! You mustn't leave me!'

A tube pulled free from his arm and blood dribbled to the floor. Wires strained against tiny monitoring pads, some breaking, others tearing free as Carter lunged forward, hands lifted, reaching for the woman. He stumbled and a panel of instruments fell with a crash.

'Helena!' Mathias, startled by the noise, came racing forward, a hypogun in his hand. 'What's happening?'

'Hallucinatory shock. Sedate him, quickly!'

She retreated as again Carter lunged towards her, his expression changing as Mathias trapped his body with his free arm, his other hand rising with the hypogun to blast a charge of drugs through his skin, the fat beneath, into the bloodstream itself.

'Arra! Ar . . .'

'He's gone!' Mathias, with practised skill, eased the limp figure back on the couch and automatically began to replace the transfusion tubes and monitors. 'He'll be out for hours. Helena, what next?'

She didn't answer, not even hearing him as, taking the commlock from her belt, she snapped at the face which appeared on the screen.

'Get me the Commander immediately!' A moment then, 'John, I must see you at once.'

'You're not still worried about that radiation exposure?' Koenig frowned. 'I told you all precautions were taken and there's nothing to be concerned about.'

'This is important, Commander!' She deliberately used the formal mode of address. 'The safety of Alpha could be involved. I repeat—I must see you immediately!'

A lamp flashed on a panel, a meter kicked, a dial quivered, tell-tales relayed the metabolic processes of the man on the couch. Alan Carter, pilot, lost in a world of dreams, perhaps, or of oblivion. Perhaps Helena could tell but if she knew she had volunteered no information as yet and Koenig was impatient.

'Is this why you insisted I come to Medical Centre? To look at Alan undergoing treatment?'

'You know me better than that, John.'

'Then why?'

'Two reasons. The first is that Carter was and is suffering from a strong hallucination. When first he woke he mistook me for someone else. He

40

touched my hair, tried to hold me. When I moved away he became almost frenzied. Bob had to sedate him.'

'You said "was and is".' Koenig glanced at the panels of the monitors. 'Are you saying that, even though unconscious, he is suffering from hallucinations?'

'No, but what I am saying is that, should he wake now, he will not be normal as we term normality. The hallucination he obviously suffered when he saw me is still present. Look!' Helena operated the panel and pointed at the uneven lines of the encephalogram. 'That is not the normal pattern of an unconscious brain. It is not even of one in a coma. If I was simply watching the pattern and not seeing Alan I'd be willing to swear that he was awake and aware. Obviously he is not. Therefore something must have affected his normal mental condition.'

'So?'

'Whatever that was must have taken place while he was in the plasmic cloud. You were also exposed.'

'And so was Paul.'

'He stayed inside the Eagle and was protected by the shields, John. You ventured outside. I submit that you too could be affected like Alan, your senses affected in a way which you probably don't even realize.'

Koenig said flatly, 'I'm not suffering from hallucinations, Helena. And I haven't time to waste in idle speculation. Victor has resolved how the nuclear charges are to be placed and we have to get on with the job. I appreciate your concern, but believe me, it is misplaced.'

41

She caught his arm as he turned to move away, the grip of her fingers surprisingly strong.

'I said there were two reasons for asking you here, John. Aren't you interested in the second?'

He had to be interested. No matter how mistaken he thought she might be, or how great the urgency of other matters, the safety of the base was paramount—and she had stated that safety could be involved.

And, as he knew, Helena was not given to wild or hysterical judgments.

'I'm sorry,' he said, and his regret was genuine. 'It's just that there's so much to do and so little time in which to do it. What do you want to tell me?'

For answer she led him into the diagnostic room, to a place before the enigmatic instruments, her eyes catching and reflecting little gleams of coloured light, the aureole of her hair a trap for drifting shadows.

Then lights bloomed from shaded sources and something of mystery and magic was replaced by the cold and irrefutable logic of science.

'These are the computer recordings taken from Eagle One,' said Helena. She picked up two flat discs each marked for purposes of identification. 'One is from the vessel itself and shows every move, course and velocity change since it left Alpha to the time of its return. The other is the individual biological monitor of Alan. We would normally have been able to receive them both in Main Mission but the plasma cloud made it impossible. However both records are quite definite. Now watch.'

She slipped the first record into a slot, tripped a

series of switches and lifted her hand to the stream of symbols which appeared on the read-out screen.

'See, John? Eagle One rose, steadied, made directly towards the asteroid. The malfunction became apparent—'

'I can read a recording, Helena,' said Koenig. 'But what are you trying to prove?'

'Not trying, John, merely displaying the evidence that something is terribly wrong. Alan was unconscious when you found him, right?'

'Yes.'

'And you will agree that, under no circumstances could a man in that condition operate an Eagle?'

'Of course.' He looked at her, conscious of the strain in her voice, the concern. 'But Alan could have been unconscious all the time. His locator beacon was activated and there were other things.'

'All of which have been recorded by the ship-computer. The ship was under pilot-control at all times—we couldn't take over from base, remember?' She didn't wait for an answer, none was necessary. 'John, Alan was unconscious from the moment the charges exploded.'

It took a moment for it to register, for the incredible to be absorbed and, when it did, his reaction was immediate.

'Impossible!'

'The records—'

'Must be wrong. That Eagle was manoeuvered, the engines cut, the course corrected, the beacon activated—it's all on the record.'

'There are two records, John. If you accept one you must accept both. According to the biological data it was impossible for Alan to have handled the ship. He was unconscious.' Helena fed the other

43

disc into the machine and, even though he was not a doctor, Koenig could read the evidence presented to his eyes. The heartbeat, the respiration, the encephalogram—all were those of a man in a quiescent condition.

'An apparent paradox, John,' said Helena quietly. 'Alan was unconscious and couldn't have handled the Eagle, but the ship was manoeuvered, as we know; therefore Alan couldn't have been unconscious.' Pausing she added, bleakly, 'Or something took over his body and used it as if it had been a puppet.'

The inevitable conclusion once the validity of the records was accepted.

Koenig said, 'There was nothing out there—we scanned.'

'Before the blast, yes, but after?' Helena met his eyes. 'And, whatever it was, John, is still showing its presence. Alan woke in a hallucinary state. He mentioned a name, Arra, he thought that I was someone else. John, you can't—'

The buzz of Koenig's commlock gave her no chance to end what she was about to say. Morrow's face on the screen was strained, incredulous.

'Commander! There's an alien vessel in space between us and the planet. It appeared from nowhere —and it's huge!'

CHAPTER FOUR

There was a shimmer about it, a subtle blend of moving radiance, lines which dissolved one into the other, curves, planes, surfaces which defied easy description. A fabrication which followed laws of other magnitudes, obeyed the dictates of a science based on novel premises. But Morrow had been right in one thing—it was tremendous.

Koenig tried to measure it against the graduated lines on the screens, frowning when the selected points refused to remain in place, the apparent size of the mysterious vessel altering as he watched.

'David?'

'The computer is baffled, Commander,' admitted Kano. 'From the evidence the ship is either flickering from one point to another at incredible speed or it is actually pulsating in size.'

The answer Koenig had expected. Sandra Benes was no more helpful.

'Readings are negative, Commander. Any forces involved are either so well screened that they do not radiate on detectable frequencies or the ship is using a type of power of which we have no knowledge.'

'And the planet?'

'The sensors are picking up information now that

the plasmic cloud has dispersed. There are evidences of life.'

'Atmosphere?'

'Breathable.'

Which meant that the detected life would be based on a familiar pattern of oxygen-carbon metabolisms. Plants, animals, perhaps even humans following a recognizable development. Koenig moved restlessly about Main Mission, conscious of a nagging doubt. Too many things were wrong; the sudden appearance of the planet, the traces of apparent life and the mysterious ship itself. A ship which had made no attempt to communicate and had answered none of their transmissions. A vessel which, perhaps by accident, had come to rest close to the point at which the nuclear charges had to be placed.

'I'm going to investigate,' said Koenig. 'Get me an Eagle, Paul. No crew.'

'You're going out there alone?' Bergman shook his head, frowning. 'I don't like it, John. Too much could happen.'

'And would a larger crew make any difference?' Koenig turned to Morrow. 'Make that an armed Eagle, Paul. Atomic torpedoes fitted with both direct contact and proximity fuses. Victor, you continue with Operation Shockwave. No matter what happens to me continue on schedule. Now, Paul, where's that Eagle?'

They watched him rise from the pad, the Eagle tiny against the orb of the mysterious planet, dwarfed by the tremendous bulk of the alien ship. Morrow, monitoring the Eagle, gave a running commentary.

'All systems go and in the green. Commander,

46

you'd best cut velocity now.' He frowned as he watched his instruments. 'Commander?'

'No response,' said Koenig. 'Check all functions for circuit failure. I'm switching to secondary controls.' Lamps flashed on the monitoring panels. 'Useless. There seems to be some kind of attractive field drawing me towards the alien. I can't alter course. I can't slow. I can't even fire the torpedoes. Victor, the base is yours. Good luck.'

Facing certain death and yet he was still able to think of others, of the welfare of his command. Then, as the Eagle seemed about to crash into the shimmering hull, Morrow shouted at what he saw.

'The hull! It's opening!'

An orifice suddenly gaped in the alien vessel directly before the Eagle, to swallow it, to close after it as if the thing had been a fish gulping an insect.

On the monitoring panel every light went dark.

The hum was low, like the maintained note of an organ in some vast cathedral, a thing more felt than heard. It tingled the soles of Koenig's feet, the tips of his fingers, caused vibrations to come from the catches of the restraints as he released them. Rising from his chair he stared at the screens, finding them, dark. Operating the controls brought no response. The Eagle was apparently dead and it was a miracle that he was alive.

He spun as the air-lock suddenly opened. Armed, he entered the vestibule, waited, stared at a wall which appeared beyond the outer port. The air was breathable. The wall, silver in colour, held a circular door. It opened as he neared it.

The chamber was vast, that he could sense, but

he knew it without direct evidence of his eyes or mind. The configurations baffled logical assessment and he found it best not to look too long or to stare too hard. Shadows drifted like skeins of ebon smoke dotted with pearls, interspersed with broken rainbows, writhing into new and ever more fantastic configurations.

'Welcome, John Koenig!'

The voice was deeply musical, perfectly enunciated, and yet he knew that it came from no normal throat. Here was a communication of minds needing none of the vibratory devices of tongue and throat, lips and air.

'Where are you?'

'Look and you shall see.'

Darkness moved, took form and substance, became the tall, imperious figure of a woman veiled, gloved, strange.

'Who are you?'

'I am Arra, Queen of Atheria, the planet which has terrified you and your people.'

'Arra?' Koenig frowned, remembering Carter, what Helena had said.

'Your pilot has mentioned me, that I know. It was necessary that he should be helped. But we met only in the realm of the mind, John Koenig.'

'You know my name?'

'I know all about you from the moment of your birth. Your race from the moment of its creation. We of Atheria have waited for you for millions of years, for long millennia while events took their courses and our destinies became as one. Now the cosmic scheme nears completion. Can you even begin to understand?'

'No,' said Koenig flatly. 'Our moon was blasted

from its orbit by an accident. No one could have foreseen that.'

The laugher was music, rippling, gushing like water over crystal stones. Elfin bells tintinnabulating through perfumed air.

'Oh, poor John Koenig. How you fail to grasp the scheme of things. Can you consider the universe as a living cell under the microscope of a scientist? The galaxy as one of the chromosomes which make up that cell? Your solar system as one of the genes which form that chromosome? If so, John Koenig, how small does that make you?'

'Small,' admitted Koenig. 'But I exist.'

'You do! Yes, you do!' The voice was a paen of gladness. 'And how magnificent is the part you play. Our worlds have met in the body of time and space and, having met, that to which I belong will . . . mutate. It will change, alter, take on a different form and meaning. You and I are vital droplets in the tremendous pattern of existence, fragments of the Master Plan. Within hours our destiny will have been achieved!'

Words which by their nature were limited to crude analogies, but Koenig could grasp what lay beneath them, the concepts the labels embraced. He thought of a spermatozoa, conscious of nothing but the need to survive, fighting, travelling relatively vast distances, coming to rest—and giving stimulus to the birth of a new life; a bacteria, a virus, a minute spore—all unaware of what their presence at the right time and place could do. If such things had consciousness of an individual life what would they think at being told the importance of what they did?

'Think of it, John Koenig,' Arra continued. The

gene of which I and my people are a part will mutate into a higher plane of existence. Once changed we shall continue immutable for all eternity. To dissolve, perhaps, to disperse, to seed new stars, new galaxies—but basically never changing as the particle of an atom never changes.'

'And us?'

'You shall continue. Your search will go on. Perhaps even you too will be changed—but the thing you intend, the explosion you plan, that must not take place.'

'Operation Shockwave?'

'Delicate forces are involved and those devices must not be used. This I must beg of you, John Koenig. This is why you are here with me at this moment. I can use no aggression to enforce my request. I must not use it. The contact which is to come, which has been destined for eons, has to be pure.'

Koenig said, unsteadily, 'You are asking me to do nothing. To believe you implicitly.'

'Yes.'

'I am not alone. There are others who may have different ideas.'

'But you are in command. You must do as I ask, John Koenig, and do it before it is too late. Already those you have left are thinking of attacking my vessel. Attacking, destroying, fighting—the rule of the savage which has no place at this time. I depend on you to fulfill the destiny of my world.'

And to believe, to have faith, to sit and wait and watch as a planet grew huge in the sky. To trust an alien entity. To persuade others to do the same.

'An hallucination.' Helena was emphatic. 'John, it could have been nothing else. First Alan and now you.'

'And the vessel we saw? Was that an hallucination?' Koenig moved impatiently from the group which had greeted him: Helena, Bergman, Mathias. They followed him into Main Mission where Morrow turned and smiled at him from where he sat before his console.

'Glad you made it back, Commander. When that ship swallowed you I would have taken bets that you were dead.' He sobered a little. 'Did you mean what you said about aborting Operation Shockwave?'

Koenig had called a halt to the plan the moment he had left the alien vessel. It had vanished now, disappearing as quickly as it had come, not even the enigmatic shape remaining as weight to back his arguments.

'Yes.'

'John, you can't do that.' Bergman said. 'That planet will collide with us within a few hours. Shockwave is our only hope of survival and—'

'I have made my decision, Victor.'

'Decision? Don't you mean delusion, John? This alien you claim you saw and spoke with—why only you? Why not communicate with us all—if aborting the operation is so important then why not explain why? We have the right to know. It is our lives which are involved.'

'Can't you trust me, Victor?' Koenig turned to Helena. 'Can't you?'

'In everything else, John, yes, but it is my opinion that you aren't normal. Delayed shock from radiation exposure could have caused these hallu-

51

cinations. That woman you claim that you saw. Can you honestly say that you know what she looks like?'

'No.' He met her eyes, turned to see others, met them in turn. 'I think I saw what she wanted me to see. Perhaps her real shape is something so alien it is beyond comprehension, but that is not important. I am talking of her mind. There was truth in it and hope and a great happiness. And there was worry and concern. A thing is to happen and it must take place in a certain way. Operation Shockwave may or may not work as we hope, but the energies released would be fatal to the event. I say we should abort the project.'

'And throw away our only chance of survival?' Bergman was stubborn. 'John, I've been over the figures a hundred times. It may not work as we hope, that I admit, but unless we try, that planet will squash us as we would crush an egg beneath a hammer.'

'Perhaps.'

'How can you doubt? The instruments—'

'You talk of hallucinations,' snapped Koenig. 'A nice, easy, convenient explanation for any unusual mental state you are not familiar with. But what if the patient saw exactly what he described? What if he lived in a world of visual reality and you did not? Alan was affected, but Arra saved his life. I can't forget that if you can. She saved his life!'

'We have no proof of that,' said Helena sharply. 'We have only your word.'

'And Alan's.'

'He is—'

'I know', interrupted Koenig bitterly. 'He's crazy.

Hallucinated. Deluded. He believes in a ghost—something you can't see. Well, can you see gravity? Magnetism? Ultra-violet light? Radio waves? Is a man mad because he believes those things really exist?'

'John,' said Bergman. 'Time is running out. We must get ready to detonate the charges.'

'No. We must trust Arra.'

'I disagree!'

An impasse and one which had to be quickly resolved. Koenig glanced around Main Mission, noting the positions of the personnel. Sandra and Morrow were at their stations, Kano by the computer, a scatter of others watching but taking no active part. Mathias had ordered two security men into the chamber, attendants summoned in case of violent behaviour, both armed with stun-guns. If he should order them into action what would Bergman decide?

He would side with them, Koenig guessed, and so would Helena. Their motives would be of the best, neither had any doubt but that he, like Carter, was sufferng from radiation-induced hallucinations. But if he was now defied his authority would be lost and, once gone, it could never be wholly regained.

And, if the others used force to abrogate his command, it would be mutiny. Something he could never forgive or forget.

Koenig said, casually, 'Time to detonation, Paul?'

'Readings, Sandra?'

'Six minutes, Commander.'

She, like the others, relaxed as she answered. 'As before, sir.'

'Fluctuation?'

'None.'

53

'I see.' Koenig nodded at the answer, then moved towards his office. 'That should give you cause for thought, Victor. While you're pondering on the significance of the lack of fluctuation I'm going to get a drink.'

A rare bottle was kept in the lower drawer of his desk, as the professor knew. A small laser pistol was clipped above it, which was Koenig's secret. He loosened it, helped himself to a drink, turned to face Main Mission as Morrow checked the time.

'Three minutes.'

'Arm the trigger.' Koenig set down his glass and, laser hidden at his side, moved towards the console. As Morrow completed the operation he lifted the weapon. 'Now get up and move to the far side of the room, Paul. Move!'

'John!'

'Shut up, Victor! I know what I'm doing. You two security men—outside. Move!'

One made the mistake of going for his stun-gun. His arm fell, smoke rising from a neat hole in his sleeve.

'Attend him, Mathias.' Koenig gestured with the gun. 'All of you, and that includes you, Helena, all of you stand well clear. Time, David?'

'One minute.' Kano was sweating. 'Commander, for God's sake—'

'It's too late!'

There was nothing to do but wait now. To rush Koenig, to chance the laser, to overpower him would take too much time. In the screens the huge expanse of the approaching planet seemed to writhe like the surface of a tormented sea. It filled the space windows, bathing Main Mission in a cold, lambent glow, accentuating features and deepening eyes so that, like waxen images they stood, waiting. They were as flies watching the fall of the hammer which would pulp their lives, their world.

Insects on the face of creation.

Something flickered.

A flash of light, a momentary darkness, light again, a blur of nights and days, the flash and whirl of an illuminated, spinning wheel, a stroboscope.

A jerk.

Nothing.

Nothing but a tiny orb far in the distance.

'It's gone!' Morrow's yell held an hysterical relief. 'The planet's gone!'

'But how?' Bergman stared up and around, incredulous. 'We saw it, the instruments registered it, and yet it's vanished.'

Moved, passed on, transmuted into something new and strange, lifted by the catalytic influence of Alpha into another type of material. Motes passing in the infinity of the universe. Minute scraps of life interacting and fulfilling an unknown destiny.

Arra had known—and Koenig had believed.

Helena came to him, resting her hand on his arm, her eyes filled with regret.

'John, I'm sorry. I should have trusted you, but I didn't know.'

'You did right, Helena. You operated on the basis of known data.' Koenig looked at the gun and slipped it out of sight. 'But Victor should have guessed.'

'Guessed what?' Bergman had heard. His face cleared as he realized what he had missed. 'Of course, John. The instruments. They should have fluctuated as we approached but they didn't. And all the time I thought you were deluded by an alien who had taken over and conditioned your mind.'

'I don't understand,' said Helena. 'What had the instruments to do with it?'

'If a man can be deluded into believing lies then so can a machine. If eyes can see what isn't there then instruments can register false data—if you have the science needed to accomplish it. Don't you understand, Helena? The original explosion when we destroyed the asteroid weakened the fabric of space and something came through from a different dimension. A living thing which saved Alan's life. A creature about to metamorphosize into something else as a caterpillar changes into a moth.'

'Arra?'

A name, a label for self-identification, but it was as good as any. She had called herself a queen—of a hive? Or had she borne within her body the seeds of a new race? Words and analogues had only touched the reality. The shape she had worn, the chamber in which she had sat, the huge vessel, the colossal world—all had been other than what they had seemed.

She had been a creature struggling to survive, one vulnerable to the projected blast of nuclear devices, one who had trusted a man and been trusted in return.

'John?'

Helena was at his side, staring up at him, her eyes a little envious, a trace disturbed. He had been distant, travelling with a being impossibly remote in space and time, remembering the voice, the singing happiness, the hope and joy.

'Sorry.' He smiled down at the woman and gently

touched her hair, her cheek. 'Yes, it was Arra, and she's left us a gift.' He pointed at the tiny orb. 'That planet. I think she copied the illusion from data received from it. In that case it could support life.' His voice rose, strong, commanding. 'Paul, I want an investigation team to check that world as soon as we are within range.'

CHAPTER FIVE

The animal was small, furtive, eyes darting from side to side, pointed ears quivering as it stared from the shadow of a clump of fern at the strange thing which had entered its environment.

A hard, metallic construction, ridged and ribbed, modules joined, giving it the appearance of a monstrous insect.

It lay in the centre of a clearing, the fronds of soaring trees rising in a ragged circle all around, leaves casting moving shadows in the brilliant heat of the day. A bird gave a rasping cry, another answered and there was a flash of gaudy plumage. Cautiously the animal crept forward. It was curious, as always hungry, and the open door at the side of the Eagle yielded unusual and tempting scents.

A sudden dart and the creature was beside the hull. Another and it stood on the edge of the open door. Snout lifted, ears pricked, it sniffed at the air.

Sniffed and ran as a voice came from the control panel.

'Come in Eagle Six. Report your situation. If you read me answer. Come in Eagle Six.'

High above the surface in his seat before the console in Alpha base, Morrow scowled at the lack of response. Irritably he tried again.

'Come in Eagle Six. You are ordered to report immediately.'

'Check the systems,' said Koenig and, as Morrow obeyed, glanced around the busy activity of Main Mission. 'Anything new, Sandra?'

'No, Commander. Temperature rising a little and humidity is what you'd expect in a sub-tropical climate. Some evidence of electrical storms in the lower left quadrant but they are too far away to affect the landing party.'

She sounded enthusiastic. Retha, the name they'd given it, was a promising world and offered a potential home. It would be even more appreciated after the recent dangers they'd survived, and Koenig would be the first to approve the exodus should the preliminary investigations work out.

Now, for some reason, the team was failing to answer.

'Any trouble with the systems, Paul?'

'None, Commander.'

'Then try again.' Koenig turned as Helena and Bergman came towards him. 'Have you completed the spectroscopic analysis of the atmosphere, Victor?'

'It checks out high in oxygen, John, otherwise it is almost identical to that of Earth.'

'Almost?'

'There's a line in the spectrum which is unfamiliar,' said Helena. 'Victor and I have been working on it. As far as we can determine it is a rare earth element in a novel combination with one of the trans-uranic elements. That's unusual enough in itself; radioactive decay would have debased any of the truly heavy elements early in the life of this world.' She glanced at Morrow. 'Is something wrong?'

Morrow spoke before Koenig could answer.

'Come in Eagle Six. Come in immediately. Report your situation.'

'John, what's happened?'

I don't know what's happened,' said Koenig. 'That's the trouble, Helena. All I know is what hasn't happened. A seven man reconnaissance party hasn't returned when it should have and they haven't checked in for the past two hours.'

'Malfunction?'

'No. According to the instrumentation all systems are in the green.' Koenig made his decision. 'Paul, bring it up on slave control.'

Morrow hesitated. 'Those people could have run into trouble, Commander. One or more of them could be hurt. They could be relying on the Eagle.'

'They could also have obeyed routine landing procedures and maintained contact,' snapped Koenig. 'I don't want to punish them, Paul, but I do want to discover what has happened. That Eagle might be able to tell us. Bring it up.'

As Morrow reached for his controls Koenig added, to the others, 'I'd like you to help me check it out when it docks. And we'd better have a few armed security men standing by just in case.'

The guards weren't needed. No savage animal sprang through the air-lock when it opened and, as far as Koenig could see, the passenger compartment was deserted. He gave it one glance then moved quickly into the command module.

Bergman said, 'No sign of a struggle, John.'

'No,' Koenig moved to the panel and checked the controls. Switches closed beneath his hands and he watched the movements of dials. 'Power full, fuel plentiful, air and essential supplies as they should be. The controls were set as would be expected after a normal landing. Nothing unusual at all. As far as I can see the crew just got up and left.'

'Leaving the lock fully open.' Bergman frowned as he considered it. 'That was wrong. The party had to investigate but they should have left one man behind in order to maintain link-contact and he should have been sealed against the environment. Was the commlock relay functioning?'

'Yes—which means that seven people apparently didn't receive our calls, chose not to answer them, or were unable to do so.' Koenig frowned. 'Two hours, Victor. That means they could have moved a distance of several miles from the landing site of the Eagle and—' He broke off as Helena called out, 'What is it?'

'Here, John! Quickly!'

She was in the passenger compartment, looking at the space between two seats set towards the rear. A spot which could not be seen at a casual glance. She pointed as the others joined her.

'Look!'

A man lay between the seats. He was stained and grimed with mud and soil and what appeared to be dried blood. His skin was roughened and creased. He wore tattered pelts and had strips of hide wrapped around his feet.

He was a savage. A man from the Stone Age. He smelt and he was dead.

Sandra Benes checked her instruments and made a notation on the automatic log. Retha had gained in surface temperature and, as was to be expected, the humidity had kept pace with the rise. From earlier reports she had a good idea of what the terrain below looked like and she had seen pictorial records of the Amazonian forests. A world of lush growth, sultry heat, moist air and exotic animals. Birds with brilliant plumage, odd cries, beady eyes which shone like gems in leafy shadows.

She had a momentary picture of what she would look like in such an environment. Skins, sandals, the bare minimum of clothing. She would let her hair hang loose and revel in the touch of rain and wind on her naked skin. And, of course, there would be a man. Carter if she had a choice. She liked the pilot and she knew that he liked her.

As if answering a mental summons he was suddenly at her side.

'Like a trip, honey?'

'Where to? The lower fungi beds in section eight? No thanks, Alan, I've seen them.'

'How about Retha?' He smiled at her expression. 'This is official. The Commander's mounting a relief expedition and I've got to maintain aerial contact and run a survey. You're a good photographer so—how about a trip?'

'Alan! You mean ride down with you?'

'That's just what I mean.' His smile widened. 'It

isn't a pleasure trip, but I guess we can squeeze some fun out of it. Get your equipment and be at the boarding point in fifteen minutes for the final briefing.'

Koenig was serious as he addressed the assembled members of the team.

'This is a full scale rescue operation. As you know the initial team appear to have vanished. Our job is to find out what happened to them and we will operate as follows. Eagle One will make a landing while Eagle Two, piloted by Carter and with Sandra making a photographic record, will scan the area for a radius of a hundred miles from the point of landing. The ground party will consist of a co-pilot, security guards, a full medical team under Doctor Helena Russell, two radiographers and a geologist. I shall be in personal command.'

Sandra said, 'About the photographic record, Commander. You want me to use full-coverage film?'

'Yes. Ultra-violet, infra-red, thermographic and spectroscopic. Try and alternate the same scene on various films and run a series of filter-shots. Alan, you will maintain a constant watch for any unusual signs of life with special reference to savages. We know they are down there and we know they could be close. Any questions?'

A man said, 'Commander, how long do we have before Retha is beyond exodus-range?'

'Three days.'

Another said, 'What about that body which was found in Eagle Six, Commander?'

'Male, weather-beaten, about middle-aged and dead.' Koenig was abrupt. 'Think of a cave-man and you've got a picture of what he looks like. As yet we don't know what killed him, but Doctor Mathias is working on the body now. The thing is that we can't afford to wait on his findings before going after the others. We've only got three days to complete evacuation if Retha is suitable and that means we have no time to waste.' His voice hardened a little. 'But I want no one to take any dangerous risks. Search procedure will be detailed on the way down. Alan, you'd better get moving.'

'On my way, Commander.'

'Good. The rest of you take your positions. Helena, check your team—we leave immediately.'

It was good to breath natural air again, to catch the scent of growing things, to hear the stir and rustle of leaves, the passage of birds. Helena stood outside the open door of the Eagle and kicked at the dirt and watched as the rich loam flew from the impact of her boot. An insect moved quickly from the disturbed soil, its carapace glinting like gemmed metal. A flash and a bird had swallowed it, vanishing as swiftly as it had struck, only a memory of shimmering wings remaining of its passage.

Above, in the sky, another bird flew, a man-made Eagle which swept across the area to circle, to bank and return.

It began to speak.

'Eagle Two to base. Am commencing search pattern. Heading north on first leg of north-east sector, check-system gamma, altitude constant over terrain.'

'Base to Eagle Two. Acknowledged.'

Morrow's voice came from the panel in the grounded Eagle, a comforting link with civilization and familiarity. Should it be broken, should they all be stranded ...

Helena shook herself, wondering at her thoughts. Retha held great potential and would possibly make a good home. Why did she feel afraid of it? Was it reluctance to leave Alpha, perhaps? In many ways the base was a kind of womb; it had held them safe and secure for a long time now. Would others also feel reluctant to leave the complex?

'Helena.' Koenig was at her side. He had stepped from the Eagle and was checking the sky, the sun. 'You look thoughtful—something on your mind?'

'This.' Her hand lifted, waved, embraced the planet. 'A big change, John, if we move.'

'If?'

'You want us to move, don't you?' She turned to face him, her eyes serious. 'You want to leave Alpha and settle down and stop having to worry every moment of every day as to the safety of the base, of what the next day might bring. But, John, once we leave there will be no going back. We have to be certain that we've made the right choice.'

'And?'

'Time,' she said. 'There isn't enough time. A whole world to be checked and only hours to do it in. It's asking too much, John, taking too great a gamble. Those others—what happened to them? Why didn't they keep in touch? How can we be sure that what happened to them won't happen to us?'

'We can't, Helena—but all life is a struggle. You of all people should know that.' He rested his hand on her shoulder, the fingers pressing with a warm intimacy, giving her some of the strength of his resolve. 'We must do what we can. Now let's go and find the rest of the party.'

They had followed the path left by the original team, the trail blazed with orange arrows spiked to trees, the orange now accompanied by others of blue. Broken twigs and crushed leaves showed the passage of several figures and footprints in the dirt held a film of moisture.

Koenig's commlock buzzed. 'Yes?'

The face of the co-pilot appeared on the screen. The man was swearing, traces of dirt on one cheek, his hair rumpled.

'We're nearing a patch of mist, Commander. The trail heads into it. Do we follow?'

'Yes. Take full security precautions. Any trace of the original party yet?'

'Just the arrows and a handkerchief one of them must have dropped. No signs of a struggle or disturbance of any kind.'

'Animal tracks?'

'None.'

'Signs of savages? No? Well, remember they could be around.'

Koenig clipped the commlock to his belt and moved on, Helena at his side. She paused, looking at a flower, an orchid-like growth the size of a plate. Beneath it a clump of fern moved.

As Helena sprang back Koenig fired.

He'd aimed at the ground, not at the fern. Threads of vapour rose from the hole the laser had punched in the damp soil. Behind the fronds something moved and crashed heavily away.

'John!' Helena was trembling. 'What was it?'

'An animal of some kind.' Koenig looked around, gun in hand. The air had grown thick with tendrils of mist, streamers coiling overhead, drifting lower, veiling the sun and sky. The birds had fallen silent and the air held a strange eerieness.

'Something is happening, John.' Helena came close to where he stood. 'Perhaps we should be getting back to the Eagle.'

It lay behind, hidden by trees and mist, but within easy reach. Koenig holstered his gun and lifted the commlock from his belt.

'Hogan? Answer me, Hogan.' The screen remained black; the co-pilot was not responding. Frowning, Koenig pressed a button. 'Alan? Do you read me?'

'Yes, Commander.' Carter smiled from the screen. 'Having a nice time down there?'

'No.'

'Is something wrong? Haven't you found the others yet?'

'Not yet. Report on local conditions.'

'A large patch of mist is close to where you are standing. It has probably engulfed the others of the forward search party by now. There are other patches drifting over the jungle. They look a little like clumps of smoke but they aren't dissipating. From up here they look a little like small, compact clouds.' He added, 'It will be dark soon.'

'I know. Get base to try and make contact. Keep overhead and ride low.'

Morrow frowned as Carter relayed the message.

'I've been trying, Alan, but I can't get any response. Can you make a visual check?'

'No. The mist is too thick.'

'Then I'll have to keep trying. If you manage to make contact order a retreat to the Eagle.' Morrow threw a switch. 'Commander we—Commander? Base calling Eagle One. Come in Eagle One.'

'Something wrong?' Bergman, his face anxious, joined Morrow at the console.

'We've lost contact with the search party.'

'And John?'

'We've lost contact with him too.' Morrow was grim. 'Even the Eagle doesn't answer. Everything's dead down there—and it's getting dark. Orders, Victor?'

'Get me Eagle Two, Paul.' As Carter's face appeared on the screen Bergman said, 'Trouble, Alan, but we don't know what kind. All contact has been lost with the others. How do you feel about spending the night on Retha?'

'On or over?'

'On. I want you to land close to Eagle One. Do nothing until dawn unless contact is made or there is an emergency. I'll send a back-up team down as soon as possible.'

They would hunt, search, try to solve the mystery if possible, abandon it if it wasn't. The men and women lost on this strange world, unable or unwilling to communicate were important but nothing could stop the moon's steady progress through space. They had only hours in which to find them.

CHAPTER SIX

It had been a pleasant break in routine and Sandra had enjoyed every moment of it. Only the missing personnel had cast a cloud over the evening and, as Carter had pointed out, they couldn't be far. With a signal light flashing from the hull of the Eagle, the receivers set on automatic, they had done all they could.

And it was a wonderful chance to be alone.

To be alone and to talk about the old days, the early hopes and fears, their lives since they had so drastically changed.

'I thought you were in love with Paul at one time,' said Carter. 'I used to be jealous of him.'

'I was—are you still?'

'No.'

'That's good, Alan.' Sandra grew serious. 'There's no room for that kind of emotion at the base. Nor anywhere, I suppose, but old habits die hard. Maybe we'll all revert back to what we used to be like once we settle down somewhere. Here, perhaps?'

'Maybe.'

'On a farm growing crops and raising animals?'

'Can you see me as a farmer?'

'We'll have to raise something, Alan. Children, then?'

'Children.' His touch was tender. 'Yes, Sandra, lots of children.'

Later they had slept and she had dreamed of a white house with neat railings and a smooth lawn over which birds glided with sparkling, colourful wings.

Waking, she stretched.

'Alan?'

She opened her eyes at the lack of an answer and saw the place where he had settled empty, his duvet thrown aside on the floor of the passenger compartment. Her own joined it as she rose and went into the command module. Carter was no-where to be seen. Sitting in the pilot's chair she unclipped her commlock.

'Eagle Two to Carter. Eagle Two to Carter. Where are you, Alan?' She relaxed as his face appeared on the screen. 'So there you are. What are you doing?'

'Just having a look round. You were asleep and it seemed a pity to wake you, so I figured I'd make a quick recce. The air's clear, no mist, and the sun is warming things up nicely.'

'Find anything?'

'Not yet. I've found the trail they marked with coloured arrows and I'll follow it for a bit.'

'Be careful, Alan, and don't be long.'

'Don't worry, Sandra. I'm a big boy now.'

Carter smiled as he broke the connection. She was quite a woman in more ways than one and he was lucky that she liked him. He lost the smile as he pressed on, his eyes wary, ears alert for the slightest sound. From all sides came the murmur of life; bird-calls, the stridulation of insects, small rustles in the undergrowth and, once, a crashing which sent his hand flying to the butt of his laser.

Drawing the weapon he stood listening, catching a hint of movement, a glimpse of something man-like lower down the trail.

'Hey, there!' Carter ran forward, lifting the gun. 'You there! Hold it!'

The ground vanished from beneath his feet.

He fell, catching a glimpse of smoothed dirt, the sides of the pit which a thin layer of fronds had covered, and cursed himself for a fool. He had been skilfully lured, the man-like thing attracting his attention, causing him to look up instead of down. Now all he could do was to twist so as to break his fall. He landed heavily, the back of his head thudding against the side of the pit, his legs squelching in mud.

Groggily he climbed to his feet.

The edge of the pit was too high for him to reach and his gun was lost somewhere in the mud, but he had hands and feet and a thinking brain. Holes could be gouged from the dirt and a series of holds made up which he could climb. As he reached up to tear away more soil he froze, looking at the faces which appeared against the sky looking down at him, the men they belonged to.

Three men, all savages, one armed with a spear.

It was a rough wooden shaft tipped with a stone flaked to a point, a crude weapon but effective at close range. Carter dropped, backing as the jagged point lanced towards his face.

'Hold it! I'm a friend! Friend, understand?'

The man with the spear snarled, lifted it, threw it with a jerk of his powerful arm. Carter lunged aside just in time; the spear slammed into the dirt before which he had stood. As he tore at the weapon its owner sprang into the pit after it.

A clenched fist smashed against the side of Carter's head, a blow which sent him reeling, dazed and almost unconscious. Releasing the spear he kicked out, felt the jar as his boot made contact, and followed it with a punch to the stomach. It was like hitting a stone wall. Before he could strike again the savage had knocked him down, torn free the spear and, lifting it, poised it to thrust the point into Carter's chest.

The commlock buzzed before it came down.

'Alan?' Sandra was impatient. 'How much longer are you going to be? Alan, answer me!'

The spear lowered as the savage leaned forward to snatch the instrument from Carter's belt. He stared at the girl's face, at his companions, then back at the face again. One thick finger rose to touch the screen, a broken nail making a thin grating noise as he passed it over the picture.

One of his companions snarled, beating at his chest, and the savage in the pit snarled back. Lifting his spear he waited until the others had caught it and almost ran up the side of the pit, holding the spear in one hand, the commlock in the other. Together they stared at the face of the girl on the screen and then, as if one, turned and ran down the trail towards the grounded Eagles.

Carter groaned, sitting upright, lifting one hand to his head. The light hurt his eyes and the faces before him were blurred.

'Give him another dose,' said Bergman. 'I don't think there are any skull fractures but there is obviously some concussion and the results of shock. Alan, snap out of it, man!'

'My head!'

'The pain will ease in a few seconds. David has given you a double dose of triphilyene-X. Now can you tell us what happened?'

'Victor!' Carter tried to stand upright, felt himself restrained by Kano. 'And you, David. What's going on?'

'That's what we'd like you to tell us,' said Bergman. 'Sandra reported that you had failed to maintain contact. We were already on our way so we lost no time, but when we arrived we found no sign of life and started looking. You were lying on the edge of a pit.'

'The edge?'

'Yes, about three feet away from the rim. From the look of it you'd torn down soil and dug yourself out. You had no gun or commlock.'

'The gun's in the mud somewhere.' Carter frowned, remembering a time of nightmare in which he had dug and clawed and fought his way upwards. He must have won free, crawled clear and then collapsed. 'The commlock? I don't know. I don't remember Sandra calling, but I could have been unconscious at the time. Those savages weren't gentle.' He described them and explained what had happened. 'I don't know why they didn't kill me—it must be my lucky day. I guess Sandra was worried.'

'When she called in, yes, Alan, she was.'

'You'd better let her know you've found me.' Carter looked at their faces and reared to his feet. This time no one tried to stop him. 'Wait a minute! You said that, when you landed, you saw no sign of life. But Sandra—'

'She was missing, Alan,' said Bergman gently. 'She wasn't anywhere to be seen.'

'Sandra? Gone?'

'Steady!' Kano caught the pilot by the arms. 'There's no sense in going off half-cocked, Alan. We've got to think this thing out. If she was taken then we'll find her.'

'When?'

'Soon.' It would *have* to be soon, but Kano didn't mention that. 'Now let's get you back to the Eagles and get rid of some of that dirt.'

For a moment Carter stood poised and then, recognizing the sense of the advice, nodded. Without a gun, without any means of communication, he would be quickly lost and could do Sandra no good. If she was dead then haste was unnecessary. If she was alive then it would only be a matter of time before he found her.

And, when he did, those responsible would pay.

'It must have been those savages,' he said when, later, in the Eagle, washed and with clean clothes, armed and equipped, he sipped at a cup of coffee. Bergman had insisted that he eat and drink. And there was time for both. Outside the ranked Eagles men were busy scouting the terrain. 'There were three of them, as I told you. Big, strong, rough characters. But how could they have managed to get into the Eagle?'

'They couldn't,' said Kano. 'Sandra must either have let them in or she had gone outside.'

'And it must have happened after she called us,' said Bergman. 'Now let us speculate a little. Those savages could have taken your commlock, Alan.

Sandra said that she had called you and her voice may have distracted them from killing you. They would have seen her face, but until they pressed the button she wouldn't have heard or seen them. Now we know they are possessed of rudimentary intelligence; the construction of the pit and the flaking of the stone tipping the spear proves that. They could have worked out that the face on the screen and the Eagles were connected. They may have seen you leave the ship, Alan, and deduced that the woman had remained inside.'

'Where she would have stayed, Victor. Sandra was no fool. She wouldn't have opened the doors to that bunch of primitives.'

'Bear with me.' Bergman rubbed thoughtfully at his chin. 'I am trying to separate what happened to the others from what could have happened to Sandra. I do not think the two things are similar—and yet the disappearances are the same.'

'It could have happened like this,' said Kano. He set aside his cup and lifted his own commlock from his belt. 'Let's assume that, after calling us, Sandra again tried to contact Alan. The savage who held his commlock could have held it like this.' He gripped his own so that the scanner pointed at the floor. 'When she spoke his hand may have tightened and his finger hit the button. Now, if it did, all Sandra would have seen would have been the ground moving past. If they were close she might have seen a flash of an Eagle. She could have thought that Alan was ill or hurt or she could have been so pleased to make contact that she didn't stop to think. She ran outside or opened the door and—'

'They got her,' said Carter bleakly. 'Those sav-

74

ages got her and took her somewhere. But where?'
He looked at them, his eyes baffled. 'I checked
this entire area and saw no sign of a village or
encampment. For God's sake, Victor, where could
she be?'

It had been a nightmare, the sudden hope so
quickly dashed, the shock of seeing the savages, the
stench, the bestial snarls, the irresistible strength
which had swept her up and flung her over a shoulder, the blow which had sent her senses whirling
into darkness when she had tried to fight.

A casual cuff without malice.

A lesson from her new master.

She watched him where he stood in the light of
a fire, a heap of glowing embers burning in a surrounding ring of stone. Smoke from the fuel rose
to coil under the roof of the cavern, joining other
smoke from other fires. Between them men and
women sat, eating, teeth tearing at barely cooked
meat, lips sucking at the marrow of juicy bones.

Men and women but no children; if any existed
they were out of sight, possibly in a separate cavern.

Sandra could not eat. She looked at the bone
the man who had taken her had thrown towards
her, the meat red, stringy, dripping with fat. The
harvest of his spear, she thought, looking to where
he stood leaning on the weapon. It gave him a
status the others did not have; they were armed
with clubs made of branches, a few with staves
holding lashed stones. To one side of the cavern
gaped an opening adorned with daubs of red pigment and skulls held to the rock by globs of dried
mud. The floor before it was smooth and a fire

burned more brightly than the others. The cave behind the opening held a pale glimmer as if a second fire, much smaller, lay within.

The abode of the leader, she guessed. The palace of a Stone Age king.

Already, even in a society as primitive as this had to be, rank and privilege were making themselves obvious.

Would her master—the Spearman—have to present her to the court? Would he have to defend her or fight 'to retain possession of her? In this crude association of peoples would a woman have any rights at all?

She knew the answer to that—none.

Here only muscle power counted, brute force and vicious savagery. Pressed, she could find the latter, but nothing could give her the physical bulk necessary to beat any of the men to the ground. The blows which alone would command respect and obedience.

Among these primitives she was a serf, a chattel, a thing to be used.

Spearman took a step towards her, grunting as he gestured at the bone she held, the food she hadn't been able to force herself to touch. A man standing to one side suddenly ran forward, snatched it, tried to escape with his prize. Spearman roared, chased him, smashed him down with a single blow of his hammer-like fist. Picking up the fallen meat he carried it to where Sandra sat and offered it in a soiled and grimed hand.

An ape offering a civilized woman a morsel of fruit.

A bribe?

A gift?

Food to fatten her up for the arduous life she now had to expect, the trials and tribulations, the endless, unremitting labour, the dirt, the disease, the degradation.

Wildly she thought of a woman with whom she had once attended social classes at college. A fanatic of the simple life who preached the concept of the noble savage and advocated a return to the land. A disciple of mid-nineteenth century romantics who dreamed of Arcadia and who conveniently forgot that the simplest luxuries—heat, shelter, tender food—all had to be torn from nature as if they were trophies won in a terrible war.

And life was a war, an unremitting war of ceaseless violence in which only the strong could hope to survive. The strong, the cunning, the hard, the ruthless.

What hope did a civilized woman with all that implied have in such a world?

Spearman moved again, coming closer, reaching out with one hand to touch her foot, run the splayed fingers up her leg, to touch her thigh, frowning at the texture of her clothing.

She suffered him, looking at the barrel of his chest, the skins which covered the dirt, the glinting shape of the commlock which he had casually thrust into his clothing.

'I—that is will you give me that?' She pointed at it. 'Please?'

His stare was the unresponsive glare of an animal.

Again she tried, reaching out to touch his shoulder, letting her fingers fall, to trail over the upper torso, to touch the metal of the instrument. A snatch and it could be hers, but time would be needed to establish contact and she doubted if she would be given the time. Later, when he was asleep, perhaps, the chance would come.

Sandra gagged when, with a sudden gesture, he rammed the bone against her mouth.

'No!' She spat, tasting char, blood, grease and grit. 'I don't want it! No!'

He grunted, mouth opening, deep gutterals coming from deep within his chest. A finger jabbed at the meat, at his mouth, at hers, each in turn.

'No!' she said again. 'I can't! I—' She broke off, cowering beneath the threat of the uplifted hand, a fist which halted its downward path as a roar echoed through the cavern.

A deep-chested bellow which came from a tall figure standing before the mouth of the small, decorated cave.

CHAPTER SEVEN

He was dressed in fine skins and was now alone. Beside him, standing a little to his rear, stood a woman as finely dressed. The king and queen, thought Sandra wildly, the rulers of this savage tribe. And, obviously, she had attracted the chief's attention.

He came towards her and she rose, Spearman at her side, his eyes wary like those of a hunted beast. As the tall figure came near he stepped forward, grunting, lifting his hand, palm outwards and upheld in a gesture of rejection.

The chief snarled.

To one side a fire sprang into sudden life as flames rose from added fuel, the dancing light touching and illuminating the scene, the watching faces. It flickered on those of the chief and the woman who had followed him. Faces which, incredibly, Sandra recognized.

'Commander! Doctor Russell!'

Both ignored her.

'John! Helena! Please!'

The woman's eyes flickered once in her direction but the man didn't look at her at all. His entire attention was concentrated on Spearman. Now he lifted his hand, pointed to Sandra, to the woman and then to himself.

Spearman shook his head, his hand stabbing at the girl and then at himself.

Again the chief moved his hand, signalling his intention to take Sandra, to add her to his women, to keep her for himself.

Spearman snarled, backing, his eyes darting from side to side. As he lunged for his spear the chief darted forward, his clenched fist falling like a hammer on the other's skull. Spearman rolled, staggered to his feet and struck at the tall figure. The chief caught his arms, lifted him and, with an explosion of muscular energy, flung him into one of the fires.

Spearman rolled, screaming, beating out flames and sparks as he ran to the far side of the cavern. Before she could follow him Sandra was gripped by the woman and dragged into the smaller cave.

The chief followed, standing before the door, staring.

'Commander!' The likeness was too strong to be coincidence, yet what else could it be? 'Doctor Russell! Both of you, please help me!'

A grunted signal and the woman slipped from the cave, leaving Sandra alone with her new master. The fire within the chamber was banked against the rear wall, the stone thick with soot, the roof hidden beneath coiling smoke. The air was thick and hard to breath, odorous with the stench of pelts which lay heaped to one side, a bed towards which she was flung.

As she landed one outstretched hand touched something hard.

A stone shaped to be gripped. A primitive hand-axe or hammer which she snatched up and lifted as the chief came towards her, one hand ripping the tunic from her shoulders and torso.

As the fabric parted and fell free Sandra slammed the stone against the chief's skull.

He grunted, swayed a little, one hand lifting to guard his head. She struck again, a third time, blood staining the stone, her hand, his matted hair.

As he slumped she darted past him, through the cave opening and into the main cavern beyond. The woman was standing far to one side before a fire which she tended with handfuls of twigs. From other fires men watched the flash and sheen of her bare white skin, the mane of hair which hung loosely over her naked shoulders, but none made a move to come close. She was the property of the chief, he had fought for her and had almost killed for her. He would fight again if anyone tried to take her for his own.

Spearman was nowhere to be seen.

He must be hiding somewhere in the distant reaches of the cavern, nursing his burns and brooding over his loss. With him would be the commlock Sandra had hoped to obtain. Now all she could do was to run and hope to get back to the Eagles before the chief could recapture her.

Already he was on his way.

She caught a glimpse of him as she ran across the cavern. He stood in the decorated opening, swaying, blood dappling his face, his eyes glazed. From his open mouth came a series of harsh gutterals and his hands gestured in unmistakable sign language.

Chase her. Hold her. Bring her back.

Orders some of the men rose to obey.

The mist was a roiling wall across the path, thick, enigmatic, the silence within it eerie, foreboding. Bergman halted, staring at it, catching Carter by the arm as he made to push past.

'Steady, Alan.'

'More delay, Victor?' Carter was impatient. 'And for what this time? It's only mist.'

'Is it?' Bergman frowned. 'The original party could have walked into a cloud like that and we know for certain the rescue team did. They entered it and they stopped communicating. A coincidence, perhaps, but there could be a connection.'

'Sure there is—the savages jumped them under cover of the mist.' Carter was certain he had the answer, Kano wasn't so convinced.

'How long does it take to send an alarm, Alan? No, if the teams had been attacked we'd have known of it. I think that Victor is right to be cautious. A gas, professor?'

'That's ridiculous!' Carter pulled at his arm. 'If the teams had died we'd have found their bodies. We didn't so the mist must be harmless. Now for God's sake let's hurry! A minute could save Sandra's life.'

'And rushing things could make her death certain.' If she wasn't already dead, thought Bergman grimly, but he kept the thought to himself. 'There could be pits and other traps and a primitive spear can kill just as effectively as a laser. We'll do this my way, Alan.'

'But Sandra—'

'Is just one of many. There's the Commander and Helena and all the others, don't forget. The savages must have taken them too.' Bergman lifted the commlock from his belt. 'Attention all units. Under no circumstances enter the mist. Stay well clear and retreat if you have to. I repeat—stay clear of the mist. Now report your positions.'

He nodded his satisfaction as the voices came from the instrument. Sonic aerial scans had shown a cavern close to the east and now men surrounded the area. From all available evidence the savages were Stone Age trogdolytes—cave dwellers, and that was where they would be found.

'Right,' he said as the last report was made. 'Let's go!'

The path wound between soaring trees, between lumpish boulders and over a mass of lichened stone. Bergman frowned as he examined the minute growths, straightening to look at the trees and shrubs, watching the darting flight of a bird. Carter had no eyes for the scenery. He walked tense and alert, gun in hand, feet probing the ground before he trusted it with his weight.

Kano said, 'What are your plans, Victor?'

'Vague,' admitted Bergman. 'We don't know how many savages we're up against so we'll have to play it by ear. Once we've found the entrance we'll go in and try to spot Sandra and the others. We might be able to get them free, in which case we'll leave and the men can take care of any chase after us.'

'Why don't we just go in and shoot hell out of them?' said Carter. He didn't look at the others as he spoke.

'We're not after revenge, Alan,' said Bergman quietly. 'That can come later if necessary, but our main objective now is to save the others. If we attack by storm they could be killed by accident or from reasons of fear. With our fire-power we can hold back the savages and release their prisoners without taking more risks than we have to.' He added, flatly, 'We've no time for making mistakes.'

No time and no inclination, Bergman, coldly scientific, judged the problem without emotion. Time and effort expended to achieve a certain objective. The minimum of expenditure to gain the maximum result.

He slowed as a sloping wall of boulder-strewn rock rose before them. Mist veiled its flanks but the part before them was clear. In it gaped a ragged opening.

'In!'

He led the rush, losing ground only towards the end when Carter passed him to vanish into the orifice. Kano, more cautious, halted at the mouth of the cavern, staring inside. As Bergman joined him he said, 'It'll be best to separate, Victor, and each cover the other, right?'

'Right, but not too far apart.'

Beyond the opening lay a winding passage, the floor rough, the walls bulging and stained with mineral deposits. Bergman led the way, hearing the clatter of Carter's boots as he ran ahead, the pilot invisible beyond a turn.

'Sandra!' Bergman heard the shout, the answering cry.

'Alan! Thank God you've found me!'

She was in Carter's arms when the others joined him. The pilot held his gun aimed towards a group of savages which edged close. Bergman knocked up his arm as he fired, the beam lancing towards the roof and sending a shower of broken stone falling to rattle on the floor.

'No killing, Alan!'

'They had Sandra!'

'And could still have the others.' Bergman glanced at the sobbing, near-hysterical girl. 'Get her out of here and take her back to the Eagles. Stay clear of the mist. When you get out order the units to close in.' He glanced at the dim vastness of the cavern, the running shapes, men and women frightened by the blast of the weapon, the falling stone. 'Ask her if she saw any of the others.'

'And you?'

'David and I will look around.'

It was a journey back into time, to a period which men had once known but had long since forgotten. A harsh and brutal era when strength was all and each day brought a new challenge.

Bergman moved slowly across the cavern, noting

the fires, discarded bones, sticks and heaps of skins and pelts. His voice was that of a professor lecturing a class of attentive students.

'They already have the beginnings of intelligence, David. They are conserving food and fuel and have learned to prepare skins for comfort and clothing. Those daubs on that wall are the first beginnings of primitive artistry and, yes, see how someone was fashioning a club.' He picked up a thick branch split at one end. A flat stone lay beside it next to a pile of strips of hide. 'Flake the edges and you would have a workable axe.'

Kano said, tensely, 'Victor! Over by that wall. That opening surrounded by skulls.'

Something moved in the light of a fire, a tall, shambling figure with blood on its head and unsteady feet. Next to it, daubing it with a red pigment, stood a woman. A low keening came from between her lips as she circled the man, touching him, springling a red dust over his head, his shoulders.

'A death-rite,' said Bergman calmly. 'Such customs are common among primitive peoples. A man is sick and they sense he will die. They consider that he is already dead and will mourn his passing and decorate his body with magical powders and liquids so as to ensure his safe passage into another world before putting him into a grave or on a pyre.'

'Alive?'

'Physically, perhaps, but if he can't save himself then he isn't worth saving. Cultures such as this cannot afford to maintain the weak. The difference between life and death is small. An hour or two, a day even, what difference does it make?' Bergman narrowed his eyes as he stared at the couple. The light was poor, but there was something about the man's face which attracted his attention. 'David, doesn't he remind you of the commander?'

'A coincidence.'

'Perhaps, but—' Bergman broke off, frowning. 'Let's take a closer look.'

The woman ran off, screeching, as they neared the spot. A heap of sticks lay beside a fire and Bergman lifted a few, lighting the ends and whipping them through the air to gain a flame. Holding up the torch he stepped close to the man and stared into his face.

'David! It's John!'

'Impossible!' Kano's voice reflected his incredulity. 'John Koenig a savage? Turned into a Stone Age man in a matter of hours? Victor, it doesn't make sense.'

'A lot of what's been happening doesn't make sense,' snapped Bergman. 'Contact Carter and get him to ask Sandra if she saw any of the others in this cavern. Quickly!' He lifted the torch again as Kano obeyed, his voice changing tone to become soft and soothing. 'John, it's me, Victor, your friend. If you recognize me say something. Just nod if you can't talk. David?'

'No, Sandra saw none of the others.' Kano hesitated. 'She did say that a couple reminded her of John and Helena, but she said that it was just a coincidence.' He turned as he caught a glimpse of movement. 'Victor! Watch out!'

A spear came lancing through the air to shatter on the ground a foot to one side. An axe followed, a hail of stones. Kano fired, triggering his gun in repeated blasts which sent molten rock dripping from the roof, aiming to scare, not to hurt or kill.

Bergman grunted as an arm swept through the air, a clenched hand slamming against his chest and knocking him to one side. As the stained and shambling figure broke into a run towards the mouth of the cavern he said, sharply, 'Don't fire, David. Warn all units not to fire. We must follow and catch him.'

Fear had made the savage agile. He reached the mouth of the cavern, passed through it and was near the end of the twisting tunnel before they could catch up with him. Beyond the ground sloped to the path, mist lying thickly to one side. It moved with a sluggish life of its own, crawling over the ground like a giant amoeba, strands of fog reaching out as if they had been blind tentacles. Bergman came to a halt as he saw it.

'David, order an aerial reconnaissance of this entire area. I want all patches of mist plotted as to recent concentration and movement. Photographic record.' He reached for his own commlock. 'Attention all units. Double precautions against being engulfed in the mist. Units to the east activate sonic probes and maintain strict surveillance. No Stone Age man to be allowed to escape. Units to north and south close in as far as is safe.'

Kano nodded as he lowered the instrument.

'Paul acknowledges, Victor. He also warned that time is passing.' He glanced down the slope. 'Look at our friend move!'

The savage was loping over the ground, skins flapping, feet pounding at the rocky loam. He saw a man standing to one side, a member of the surrounding units and, turning, headed for the mist.

It closed over him like a shroud.

Closed and roiled and lifted to withdraw, revealing a limp figure on the ground.

'Victor!' Kano's yell echoed from the slope, the trees, the very mist itself. 'That's the commander!'

John Koenig, lying still, his face pale, his head bloodied with wounds.

Bergman reached him, felt his heart, the great arteries in the throat and expelled his breath with a gasp of relief.

'He's alive, David, but he needs treatment.'

'But where did he come from?' Kano shook his head, bewildered. 'I don't understand this. That savage ran into the mist, it lifted and we found the commander. What's happening here?'

'The proof of my suspicions. The mist—it has to be the mist.' Bergman lifted his commlock. 'Attention all units. Move into the cavern and clear it of all human life. Use stun-guns if you have to but under no circumstances fire to hurt or kill. I repeat—you must not hurt or kill. Get those men and women outside and head them into the mist.'

'Victor?'

'Don't you understand, David?' Bergman lowered his commlock and gestured to two men to lift Koenig and carry him to the waiting Eagles. 'There aren't any real savages. There never were. Those Stone Age people we saw, the ones which took Sandra —they are all members of the missing teams!'

CHAPTER EIGHT

Mathias grunted as he made the final check and slapped Koenig on the shoulder.

'You'll have a sore head for a while, John, but that's about all. No signs of regression or any other physical abnormality. The rest are the same, all as good as new.' He sobered a little. 'All but one.'

Sandos, who had ridden up with the Eagle and had been found dead.

Koenig shook his head as he thought about it. He had seen the films and studied the records, but even now the whole episode seemed incredible. As the last of the men and women who had been examined left the Medical Centre Koenig moved towards the desk, fitted a spool into the replaying machine and switched it on.

The viewpoint was from above; the film had been taken from an Eagle, so the depicted figures were foreshortened and oddly distorted. Even so there was no mistaking their savagery.

A bunch of Stone Age trogdolytes, herded from the cavern and driven into a writhing cloud of mist by wary security units. A mist which had embraced them and then had lifted to move on, leaving the ground littered with unconscious figures. The men and women who had formed the investigation teams.

Eagles had lifted them back to Alpha, where they had been examined and tested and, now, re-checked for any latent abnormalities.

'Still puzzled, John?' Bergman had come to stand beside Koenig at the desk.

'Yes'.

'And so am I.' Helena joined the group. 'I can remember what happened. We walked into the mist and then, suddenly, we were on an Eagle being lifted back to base. What happened in between is a mystery. I've tried to remember, but all I get are vague impressions of what seem to be dreams.'

'The mist,' said Koenig. 'You were right, Victor, the mist was to blame. But what made you suspect it?'

'It didn't act right, for one thing.' Bergman reached out and changed the spool in the machine, fitting another. 'This is a speeded up photographic record taken with radio-sensitive film and using Al-tarve filters. Now watch.' On the screen a lumi-nescent blob moved with a rippling motion over the terrain around the site of the cavern. 'Familiar, Helena?'

'It's like an amoeba.'

'Yes, and it's alive.' Bergman switched off the machine. 'Alive in a way I can't as yet even begin to understand, but it certainly is far from being a harmless mist. That strange element we discov-ered—I found it to be concentrated in the mist patches, and there were other abnormalities. Small things, but they made me suspicious; lichens of a type which didn't belong in that environment, an oddity about the trees, a bird—' He broke off,

90

shrugging. 'Call it an inspired guess. Perhaps I was just lucky, but the mist was the only thing which could account for the disappearances. Even at that I was slow—the evidence was before us all the time.'

'Sandos?' Koenig frowned. 'The autopsy proved nothing other than that he had simply died of heart failure.'

'But his presence in the Eagle proved a lot more.' Bergman glanced from one to the other. 'It was so obvious we just didn't see it. Sandos was the duty pilot and he didn't desert his post as we first thought. The mist engulfed the Eagle and he was changed. Afraid, he crouched between the seats. We called, sealed the vessel and lifted it back to base. Sandos, or the savage he had become, simply died of fright.'

'Changed,' said Helena. 'Civilized people turning into Stone Age trogdolytes. How, Victor? How?'

'I don't know,' he admitted. 'And I doubt if we will ever know. All we can do is to guess and make crude analogics. Take a tuning fork, hit it, its vibrations will set up a sympathetic harmonic in another placed close by. Perhaps the mist was a time-warp constructor and provided an opening into the past. Those taken by it could have been exchanged with others from a different time. Or you could have been sent back, your civilized knowledge erased and only the genetic memory pattern of an earlier existence left to guide your actions. Certainly had you been killed as a savage, you would be dead and stuck in that time as Sandos was. Think yourself fortunate, John, that Sandra didn't hit a little harder.'

'And that you arrived in time to prevent Helena

91

burying me.' Koenig smiled as he touched her hands. 'Why did you want to do that, Doctor?'

Her eyes met his own, direct, serious.

'I don't know, John, but it could have been because I was jealous. Even in those days a woman must have wanted to be special to a man.'

'As she is now,' he said softly. 'As she will always be.' His fingers closed over her own. 'Helena, I—'

The commlock at his belt hummed its demand for attention. It was Morrow. He said, without preamble, 'Object spotted in the north-eastern quadrant, Commander. No danger—but you might find it interesting to come to Main Mission.'

It wasn't very large and its course would carry it clear, but Koenig was intrigued. The density of the object was high for one thing and the shape was oddly symmetrical, and ovoid a little like an egg, the long axis aimed in the direction of motion.

'It's on a transit orbit,' said Morrow. 'Probably caught in Retha's gravitational field. It's on an elliptical course with the planet as one focus and the other set way, way out. Something like a comet,' he added. 'But this thing is solid.'

'The density is approximately that of lead,' reported Sandra. 'No radiation emission detected.'

'None at all?' Koenig frowned. That, in itself, was unusual. All matter had some residual radioactive electronic storms of space. 'Albedo?'

'Almost nil.'

Matter which didn't radiate and didn't reflect light and was as dense as lead. The clinkered core of some long-dead planetoid, perhaps, or a fragment tossed from the exploding heart of a ruptured sun?

Morrow said, 'It could be valuable, Commander. It's too big for us to bring down and the course is wrong for us to throw it into orbit, but maybe we could do some mining while it's within range.'

Koenig had already considered it. Heavy metals were valuable and in short supply on the moon. The nuclear charges previously used had to be replaced and, unless the sighted object was homogenous, portions of it would have to lie within the area of uranium-plus densities. Fuel for the atomic piles. A chance he couldn't afford to miss.

'Order an Eagle to be readied and set on the pad, Paul. Full mining gear and heavy-duty lasers. Victor and I will make a preliminary survey.'

'Pilots?'

'Carter has the right as head of reconnaissance. Who is next on the duty list? Baxter? Right, warn him to get ready and have Anderson stand by for refining any samples we bring back with us.'

Baxter was a tall, broad-shouldered man who had one love in life and who revelled in any chance he could get to exercise it. A natural-born flyer, he spent hours at the simulators, more hours painstakingly constructing models of ancient flying machines. A hobby with a purpose; if and when they ever found a habitable world those old machines could pay dividends in providing a cheap means of basic aerial transport.

As he so often told those he managed to get to listen, 'Eagles are fine while we have the power to operate them and the technology to make them, but what happens when we land and scatter and each family will want its own means of transport? We can't all own an Eagle. We can't build roads and we have no trucks. But the wind is free and we can make hydrogen and helium—so it'll be back to low-powered airships. You'll see!'

Now he smiled at Carter as he dropped into the co-pilot's seat and quickly checked the instruments.

'Spin you for who takes her?'

'You take her.' Carter relaxed in his chair. 'Just for once I want to be given a ride.'

It was a good one, Baxter handling the controls with easy expertise. Carefully he set the Eagle down on the surface of the ovoid and watched as Bergman took a series of readings.

'There's something odd here, John,' he reported. 'The sonic scan shows a cavity within the interior. It's a bubble set a third of the way back from the wide end.'

'A freak?'

'Possibly.' Bergman checked his dials. 'The surface is remarkably smooth, almost as if, at one time, it had been polished. And yet the albedo is incredibly low.'

'The abrasion of spacial dust could have given it that finish, Victor, and we can find out about the albedo when we analyse the composition of the material.' Koenig checked his space suit. 'I'm going out. Each of you follow at one minute intervals.

Leaving the ship Koenig was suddenly awed by the majesty of creation. He stood, looking up at the universe, the scattered stars glowing like a mass of scintillent diamonds, the points of luminous colour as if other gems had been stirred among the crystalline whiteness, alien furnaces radiating their heat and light to warm equally alien worlds.

Beneath his feet the surface of the strange ovoid curved sharply to all sides. The orb of the moon was close, like a withered, pocked old woman, scarred with time and splintered with fissures. The tremendous crater of the explosion which had forced it from its eon-old path gaped like a leprous sore.

'John?' Bergman was beside him, his voice clear over the radio. 'Something wrong?'

'No.' Koenig gestured at the sky, the stars. 'I was just looking and reminding myself just how small we all are on the scale of creation. And, Victor, if all this is just a part of a single cell—what manner of being must comprise the whole?'

Bergman said, dryly, 'Size is relative, John. What would one of the cells of your body think if it had the capacity of conscious awareness? Yet I agree that such a creature as you propose must be more than just an expansion of the normal. And yet, it too could be nothing more than a mote in the eye of an even greater being.'

As he joined them Carter said, 'Gentlemen, philosophic speculation is all very well in its place, but somehow I don't think this is it. Now—where do we start digging?'

They had power drills but the bits wouldn't bite, the adamantine metal skidding from the surface as if they were toothpicks probing ice. Koenig frowned as he examined them, changed them for others of softer metal, but the results were the same.

Sonic drills had no better luck; in the end they burned holes with lasers and filled them with explosive charges. Back in the Eagle Bergman stared his disbelief.

'John! The surface has extruded the charges! It's as if it has grown back beneath them and pushed them from the holes.'

'We'll try again.' Koenig hefted a heavy-duty lastorch. 'I'll work alone and dig a couple of holes. When they're filled I'll head back and you blow them as soon as I'm in the lock.'

A race, but Koenig wasn't trying to be precise and it was a race which he won. A section of the strange material shattered beneath the pounding of the explosives; fragments flying off into space, others rapping against the hull of the Eagle. Metal shone beneath the lights in the crater which was formed.

Metal embossed with a strange pattern.

'This is artificial.' Bergman held his light closer, the tip of one gloved finger running over the series of ridges. 'John, this whole thing could be a fabrication, a sphere of metal overlaid with that rock we blew away.'

'Age?'

'Impossible to tell. Millennia, certainly, from the appearance of the outer crust. But this pattern, it must mean something. A design in code, maybe? A message?'

'For whom? And why should it have been covered?' Baxter was standing too close. Koenig pushed him back and aside. 'Careful, Victor, we don't know what this is all about.'

But they had to penetrate the metal, to see what lay beyond. Human curiosity could not be denied and they still had need of the heavy metals the

"Serious trouble, John," Professor Bergman announces. "Sensors have spotted something massive heading directly toward Alpha."

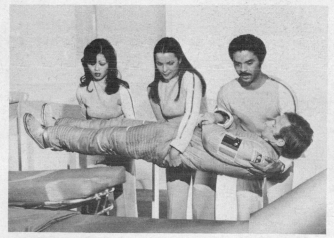

Though the Eagle's pilot is taken from his ship totally unconscious, his aircraft had been maneuvered expertly and safely back to Alpha. Could an unknown force be using him as if he were a puppet?

Armed, Commander Koenig explores the alien vessel.
The chamber is vast and filled with eerie shadows cast
by the webs of ancient spiders.

"Welcome, John Koenig," a deep nonhuman voice whispers. The darkness reveals a woman, heavily veiled. "I am Arra, queen of the planet that terrifies your people."

"Arra wasn't an hallucination, Helena," Commander Koenig maintains. "Perhaps her real form is something so alien I wouldn't have even been able to see her."

The screen reveals the huge expanse of the rapidly approaching planet. Impact within a few seconds—Main Mission Control is frozen with horror, waiting. . . .

Something moves beneath a clump of fern. Koenig fires his laser, and a thin thread of filmy vapor slowly engulfs them. It is rising from the hole his weapon punched in the strange planet's soil!

Savages, primitive but deadly, wait in ambush, armed with crude clubs and spears. Their life is a constant war, a brutal nightmare where strength alone insures survival.

A battle begins in the "castle" of the chief. With an explosion of animal energy, the tribal leader flings his opponent into the fire.

The queen of this harsh community, dressed in finer furs yet smeared with the same blood and dirt as her subjects, looks incredibly like Alpha's Dr. Russell!

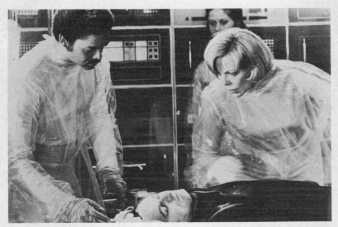

The alien's thick bandages are cut away. "Fantastic!" Dr. Russell exclaims. "An hour ago this man was crushed and dying—now just look at how he's healed himself!"

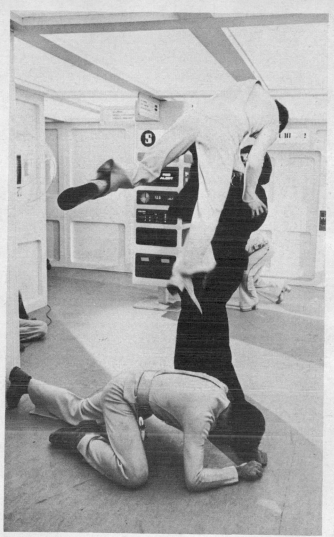

Tall and arrogant, the defiant creature stands in a corridor of Alpha. One crewman lies slumped at his feet, severely injured, while another is simply tossed out of his way.

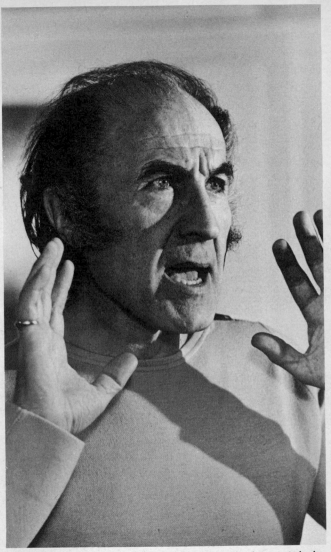

Professor Bergman cries, "The alien is immortal, indestructible! And there is absolutely no way in the universe we can stop him!"

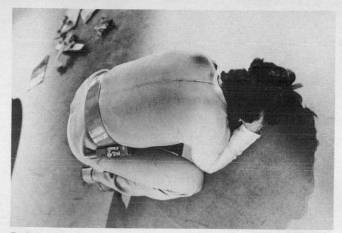

Balor, the alien, runs wild. He is determined to force the Alphans to accept him as their ruler. Helpless victims, they are the objects of a madman's greed and his desire to bring Alpha to its knees.

How to be rid of a demon who cannot be killed? The answer lies right behind a door. . . .

Flying in the Eagle to the planet's surface seems like coasting through a pillow of cotton. Yet the voices of real Earthmen keep urging them closer and closer to the face of the alien planet. Surely those below want to be rescued. . . .

The planet is an icy hell. The cold cuts like a knife, biting through the Alphans' protective clothing. They are left desperately numbed and slowly approaching death.

"Thank God they found you, John! We had given you up for lost!"

The lost men from Earth live in a palace of glittering ice. They salvaged everything they could from their demolished spacecraft, creating articles from solid rock when necessary and scattering the thick furs of animals around to serve as warm beds.

"No, we are not ghosts," the Alphans are told. "We are the survivors of the Uranus Expedition of 1985."

"Go home, Alphans!" the woman screams. "He hasn't told you the real price you'll have to pay for immortality!"

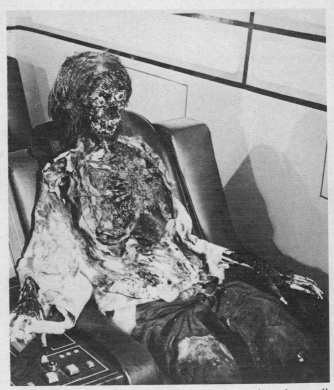

In a flash, it is all over. Years of aging take place all at once. Where Dr. Rowland sat a moment before, there remain only skeletal fragments and bits of clothing.

ovoid must contain. The metals and perhaps other things of value.

Bergman said, 'I'll try a pulsating sonic beam applied directly to the centre of the pattern. It could be a lock of some kind. Vibration might trigger it and certainly it will loosen it.' A lamp glowed on the instrument in his hands as he threw the switch. For a long moment he held it hard against the metal without any apparent result.

'The outer covering shielded it,' said Koenig thoughtfully. 'It could be actinically activated. Try a diffuse laser beam at the same time as the sonic vibrator, Victor.'

'It could be a combination,' Carter suggested. 'Can't we hook up light and sound together to cover a wide range of combinations?'

'A random-selective accelerated frequency modulator.' Baxter was certain he had the answer. 'I'll rig one up while you keep at it.'

It took him fifteen minutes and the door opened in two.

Koenig looked at the thick panel as it swung on hidden gimbals, the bars edging the jamb, the thick pads against which it had rested. A door which belonged to a bank vault rather than to any ship of space. Something designed to withstand any assault, but which had yielded to the correct combination of impulses provided by Baxter's jury-rigged tool.

Beyond it lay a passage illuminated by glowing bands set into the material of the walls, roof and floor.

Koenig entered it followed by the others and, as the last of the four passed the portal, the door swung shut behind them.

'What—' Carter turned, startled. 'Commander, we're trapped!'

'No.' Koenig stepped towards the door and tugged at it. The massive valve hesitated a moment then swung open. The balance and lack of friction were incredible. 'Automatic,' he explained. 'There must be infra-red scanners picking up our body-heat. Let's see what lies further in.'

Another door, thinner this time, but just as well built. As it closed after them the lights changed colour and a trace of dust rose to plume about their legs.

'Air.' Bergman checked his wrist-instruments. 'Pressure twelve pounds to the square inch. Oxygen, nitrogen, inert gases, hydrogen—John, we can breathe this!'

Koenig lifted his face-plate. The air was dry, a little musty, but otherwise quite sweet. The passage, obviously, was an air-lock which made the ovoid far more than it had first appeared. Beyond the door now facing him at the end of the passage must lie the hollow they had spotted, a chamber which could hold the answers to this enigma— or it could be empty—there was only one way to find out.

'Baxter, see if you can open it with your device.'

The co-pilot nodded and applied his crude instrument. A thin singing came from it, was caught and magnified by the door, the pattern it carried on its surface. The same pattern as marked the outer lock.

The singing grew higher, thinner and then, with shocking abruptness, the portal burst outward in a release of explosive forces which sent them all slamming against the sides of the passage.

'Baxter!' Koenig knelt at his side. The man had taken the full force of the blast and had been hurled back up the passage to hit the intermediate door, to fall in an untidy heap. 'Baxter?'

'I'm all right, Commander.' He rose and stood swaying a little. 'Just a bang on the head.' He straightened. 'I'm better now. Let's go and see what we've found.

A room like a sphere, the floor flattened, the sides adorned with paintings depicting scenes of torture, violence, destruction and death. Scenes from an inferno, all clear in the light which streamed from inset glowing plates.

Light which showed a wide couch and a crumpled figure. A body which was twisted, hands which were upheld, a face which they partly covered.

The body of a man with a face of a broken, tormented angel.

CHAPTER NINE

Helena checked the seals, activated a switch and relaxed as a lamp flashed on the panel of the amniotic tank in which the alien had been confined.

'That's the best I can do, John. The rest will have to wait until he's back on Alpha.' She nodded to waiting attendants. 'Take him out and use all precautions. I'll be with you as soon as you're ready to leave.'

Koenig said, 'Will he live?'

'If he does it will be a miracle. There must be terrible internal injuries and you saw how his face was cut and slashed. How did it happen?'

'The door was booby-trapped,' said Koenig grimly. 'It had to be. Massive charges had been fixed around the jamb and they blew when we opened the door. The main effect was in here, naturally, but we caught the back-blast. Baxter was hit pretty badly and I think he should be looked at.'

'He will be.' Helena stared around the chamber. 'I can't understand this. A man locked up in a tiny world, the doors sealed and rigged to kill whoever is in here when they are opened. And those pictures—' She shuddered. 'John, they're horrible! Vile! I'm a doctor and I know something about the agonies the human frame can suffer, but those things are the product of a diseased mind. Did he do them?'

'I doubt it. There are no paints.' No paints, no books, no toys of any kind, nothing to offer distraction or to alleviate the utter monotony of the truncated spherical chamber, the glowing light, the paintings. A cell, thought Koenig bleakly. A prison, certainly, and something cold ran up his spine at the thought of whoever had designed it.

'I'd better attend my patient.' Helena hesitated as if expecting him to accompany her. 'John?'

'You go ahead. I want to look around here for a while.'

Koenig began his search as Helena left. The walls, as he had found out before, were seamless, but he examined them again for a means of entry other than the door. It, like the outer port, was massive and he frowned as he mentally estimated the force of the explosion which had flung it so violently open.

An explosion which had left the chamber almost undamaged. One intended to crush the solitary occupant, but which had failed in its objective. For a time at least, Koenig had read Helena's expression and knew that she, like himself, had no hope of the alien's survival.

'Found anything new, John?' Bergman entered the chamber. He was suited and carried a load of equipment, his face behind the face plate of his helmet intent.

'Nothing new, Victor.' Koenig waited until the other had opened his helmet and switched off his suit-radio. He always found it a little disturbing to hear a double voice and more so to hear himself as an echoed ghost on the speakers when talking naturally with the radio switched on. 'Yet there must have been a way out of here other than by the door.'

'Why?' Bergman answered his own question. 'In order to maintain the life-support apparatus, naturally. There must be machines somewhere in order to maintain the lights and atmosphere and he would need to eat and drink. Unless—' He broke off, frowning. 'No. That is inconsistent.'

'What is?'

'The concept that whoever built this didn't want the occupant to live.'

'Inconsistent or illogical, Victor?'

'Both. To build a cell and not to provide its occupant with the means of survival is inconsistent with the concept of a cell, which is a place to confine someone who has done or could do you harm. And to build it in the first place when you don't intend its occupants to live is illogical.'

'By our terms, Victor,' reminded Koenig. 'But we're talking about aliens. How can we tell if their concepts are the same as ours? To us, cooping a man up like this is incredible. A proof of a sadistic bent which we find disgusting. Kill him, yes, if he deserves it. Confine him, yes, if he needs to be confined. But this torture is worse than anything thought of in the dark ages. To be locked up and left for—' Koenig frowned. 'How long did you say, Victor? Millenia?'

'That's what I thought. Obviously I was wrong.' Bergman set down his instruments. 'Would you care to help me, John?'

'No,' said Koenig. 'I want to see what luck Helena's having with our mysterious friend.'

She was attending Baxter when Koenig arrived at Medical Centre, the amniotic tank set to one side in the ward, a pulsating green light signalling the viability of the person inside.

The co-pilot sprawled in a medical chair, his head thrown back, his eyes wide as he looked into the lenses of a binocular-like instrument.

'There's nothing wrong with me aside from a slight headache, Doctor. I took a bump, sure, but that's all. I've had a dozen worse in my time.'

Helena said, 'Close your left eye. Now touch the tip of your nose with your right hand. Good. Now with your left. Fine.' She lifted the instrument and swung it to one side. Stepping over to a small table she picked up something. 'Catch!'

Baxter grabbed for the shining object, a crystal vial, and missed. He picked it from his lap.

'Thank you.' Helena took it. 'You do a lot of flying, don't you, Mike?'

'I did. I'd still like to.'

'There aren't many opportunities now, though, are there?'

'No, but there's always the routine check-flights and investigation probes when we have to make a search. And then—' Baxter broke off and then continued, slowly, 'What are you trying to tell me, Doctor?'

'We all get old, Mike, and we all change a little.'

'Not me.'

'You too. That bump did you no good. I'm going to recommend that you take things easy for a while. A desk job in Main Mission. Your experience will be valuable when it comes to correlating flights.'

Baxter rose from his chair. His face was grim, almost savage, his voice a tense accusation.

'Doctor, are you telling me that I'm grounded?'

'I'm recommending that you be given a rest.'

'From flying? Who the hell wants that?'

Koenig said, sharply, 'Get a grip on yourself, Mike! Hitting the doctor won't cure what's wrong. That was a bad fall you took and it's natural there should be after-effects. A few days and you might be fit again. For now you polish a chair and you like it.'

'But—' Baxter controlled himself with a visible effort. Swallowing he said, 'I'm sorry, Doctor Russell. It's just that you threw me a little. No one likes to be told he's being scrapped.'

103

'Not scrapped, Mike.' Her tone was gentle. 'Just rested.'

'In my book there's no difference. Have I the right to know what's wrong?'

Helena glanced at Koenig. He nodded.

'It's your eyes, Mike,' she said. 'The retinas are loosened and almost completely detached. We might be able to fuse them into place with a medical laser beam later on, but for now it's essential that you rest.'

'My eyes?' Baxter sucked in his breath. 'You mean I'm going blind?' His voice rose a little. 'Blind!'

'No,' she said sharply. 'You aren't blind and we can save your sight, given time. But any sharp blow such as you'd expect in a rough landing and you'd lose your vision. Already it's faulty—you didn't catch that vial. I'm sorry, Mike, but there it is. I can't pass you fit to fly.'

'I see.' His voice was flat, emotionless. 'Is that all, Doctor?'

Helena sighed as he left. 'You know, John, I've had to give bad news a thousand times and you'd think you could get used to it if you do it often enough, but I never have. Each time is like the first. If only there was something I could do, some hope I could give, but—'

'Baxter is a man, Helena. A flyer. He'll be all right.'

'He may survive, John, but you know better than to say he'll be all right. I've just ruined his life and you know it. Even if I can repair his eyes he'll never be able to fly again.' Helena shook herself, a woman who too easily felt another's pain, the occupational hazard risked by any doctor.

Koenig said, 'What about our alien friend?'

'I'm waiting for Bob to prepare the surgery.' Helena turned as Mathias came into the ward. 'Ready?'

'As much as we'll ever be.'

'Good.' Helena drew a deep breath. 'If you've got a lucky charm, John, you'd better rub it. We're going to need all the power it can give.'

A superstition, but he sensed that she wasn't wholly joking. It was never easy to deal with the forces of life and death and now both she and Mathias were about to plunge into the unknown.

Koenig watched as assistants wheeled the amniotic tank into the surgery, standing before a transparent partition, details sharp and clear beneath the brilliant cone of light over the operating table.

Words rustled from the speakers like dried leaves swept by an October wind. Rapid instructions which sent men to unseal the tank, to open it, to reveal what lay within.

A shape covered in crusted bandages.

'Cutters?' A nurse placed them in Helena's hand. 'I'll open this cocoon, Bob, and we'll see just how bad he is superficially. Then we'll get him on the table and rig up some kind of life-support system. If the tank maintained his life it shouldn't be too difficult—at least we're winning so far.'

Mathias lifted a hand, fingers crossed as Helena began to cut open the bandages she had applied in the amniotic chamber. They were thick with dried blood, parting slowly beneath the gleaming jaws of the cutter.

Handing over the tool to a nurse she gripped the cut edges and pulled.

And froze.

'Bob.' Her voice was strained. 'Bob—there isn't a mark on him. His face is completely healed!'

So was his entire body as far as medical science could determine. Koenig read the report and stared at Helena. Shrugging she turned to Mathias.

'Bob? Can you explain it?'

'A man crushed and dying, torn by the effects of a violent explosion, bones shattered, tissue pulped—a man who within a matter of an hour manages to heal himself? No, Helena, I can't explain it.' Pausing he added, wistfully, 'But I'd give ten years of my life to know how it was done.'

'Maybe he'll tell us.' Koenig threw the report on the desk. 'Not conscious as yet?'

'Not as far as we know.'

'You aren't sure?'

'John. as far as this character is concerned, I'm not sure about anything.' Mathias rose. 'Helena, it's time we made another check.'

Koenig accompanied them into the intensive care unit where, behind a panel, the alien lay bathed in a bluish glow. Helena checked the monitor lights and pursed her lips at what the tell-tales registered.

'Pulse strong, breathing regular, vitality factor incredibly high. Any normal person would be dead by now, but he isn't normal, certainly not in human terms.'

'What we need to know is precisely how he is abnormal,' said Koenig.

'Take your pick.' Helena gestured at the dials. 'That vitality factor, for example, is ridiculous. Even a man at the height of physical and mental fitness wouldn't register at that level. The healing process is normally a matter of accelerated cell growth—in this case the acceleration is fantastic.

And not just the production of scar tissue, John, but actual regeneration. There isn't a trace of a scar or lesion, not even a thickening of the epidermis.'

'Conclusion?'

'It's too early for that yet, John. We haven't enough data. All I can make at this time is a few wild guesses. He is an alien, that we know. Regeneration of the type he displays is, on Earth, confined to certain lower orders such as crustaceans who can grow a new claw if one is lost, or a lizard which can grow a new tail. Maybe his race managed to incorporate that secret into their metabolism or maybe they just evolved with it.'

'A handy little attribute to have,' said Mathias. 'Well, we can't do anything standing around here. We've got those computer findings to correlate, Helena, and we still have to check those slides we took from our friend. If there's nothing else, John?' Koenig took the hint.

Bergman was in his laboratory busy with a scrap of rock-like substance. He prodded it with a slender metal rod as Koenig crossed the room towards him.

'When you were a boy, John, did you ever read a story about a substance which doubled and grew and doubled and just kept on growing?'

'No.'

'A pity; as I remember, it was a great yarn. This stuff reminds me of it.'

'From the ovoid?'

'Yes. I managed to blast free a fragment from where it's starting to grow back over the door. It has an amazing structure based on a triple-bonding of mutually enhancing constituents. It isn't just crytalline and monocomposite as you would expect normal rock to be. In fact it acts almost as if it were alive.'

Koenig picked up the fragment and hefted it. It felt solid and as heavy as lead. The surface was smooth as if it had been machined.

'It's growing,' said Bergman. 'Multiplying itself as if it were a kind of yeast. My guess is that it's feeding off the very radiation present in this room. Certainly the temperature has lowered since I brought it into the laboratory. You notice how low the albedo is; the stuff doesn't reflect but sucks up energy like a sponge. Life, John, primitive and in the order of our own chemical compounds, but anything which eats, grows and perpetuates itself follows the basic pattern of survival.'

Something over which philosophers had argued in the past and would do so again in the future, but Koenig had no wish or inclination to split hairs.

'A coating then,' he said. 'Was a coating put over that ovoid?'

'Put over or gained while in transit through space,' corrected Bergman. 'However I am inclined to think it was deliberately used. Coupled with the heavy doors, the locks and the booby-trap, I think we can guess why.'

'To hide it,' said Koenig. 'To seal it in and to grow like barnacles over the original metal so that it would be impossible to recognize.' He threw the fragment back on the bench and rubbed his hand. It was chilled. 'Victor, if you wanted to destroy a thing like that how would you do it?'

'I don't know,' said Bergman, flatly. 'I don't think that it can be destroyed. It lives on energy, don't forget, and so will feed on any force you turn against it. Even if you managed to shatter it, it would grow again. A single, tiny crystal would reproduce to restore the entire mass.'

'A single crystal,' said Koenig thoughtfully. 'Or a single cell.'

'If that stuff were a man, yes.'

Koenig reached for his commlock. 'Get me security. Security? Send men to guard the Medical Centre with particular reference to the intensive care unit. They are to prevent the patient under care from leaving the area. What?' He frowned as he listened to the voice from the instrument. 'I see. Full red alert immediately. Take all appropriate action to isolate and negate the threat.'

As the alarm began to echo through the base he said to Bergman, 'Trouble, Victor. Our alien guest has run amuck.'

CHAPTER TEN

He stood at the intersection of two corridors, tall, arrogant, proud in his defiance. A man lay slumped at his feet, with two others wearing the same purple sleeve to one side. One of them moaned a little, twitching. The stun-guns he and his companions had tried to use lay where they had fallen.

'They didn't work,' said Carter. He had met Koenig as he had come running to where the alien had been found. Three jolts, enough to drop an elephant, and they didn't work.' He lifted the laser he carried. 'Shall I use this, John?'

'Give him a warning. Fire close to his head.'

The alien stiffened as Carter raised the weapon. Before he could move the pilot had fired, molten metal running from the point where the beam hit the side of the corridor inches from the stranger's head. The gun fired again, this time aimed at the floor, a beam of raw energy which could crisp and sear and burn through flesh and blood and bone.

'Wait!' The words were thick, becoming more clear as the alien continued. 'Please . . . I must communicate . . . talk with you. I am Balor, citizen of the planet Progon. I . . . the words . . .' The handsome face frowned, brows knitting as if the brain behind the lambent eyes was seeking, learning.

A form of telepathic education, Koenig guessed. If so it was highly efficient.

He said, 'Why did you attack us?'

'Commander, please believe me. I mean you no harm.'

Helena had joined the group. She said, 'We brought you here because you were injured—we wanted to help you.'

'I understand that now,' said Balor. 'But when you blasted your way into the ovoid I was hurt, disoriented. When I regained awareness I was in some kind of box, my body encased in instruments. I had to escape. Then your guards attacked me and I had to defend myself. But I am a civilized man and when weapons of destruction are used it is time to cease conflict and to talk to each other. To find a common understanding. Yes?'

'Yes,' said Koenig. 'We'll talk, but not here. Let's go into my office.'

Curious glances followed the party as Koenig led the way through Main Mission, and he could guess why. The alien dominated the scene. Taller than the others, he radiated an almost visible aura of vital power and he had already demonstrated his extreme physical strength.

The door closed, the group assembled at his desk. Koenig said, 'Balor, we could do with some explanations. First, how is it that you weren't affected by the weapons used against you?'

'The instruments designed to affect the nervous system?' Balor smiled. 'They have no effect against me. Neither would the beam you threatened me with.'

Carter said, dryly, 'It would be a mistake for you to gamble on that.'

'It would be no gamble. You wish to prove my words? Then go ahead, shoot me if you wish, I assure you that no harm will be done. My body is indestructible.'

Helena said, 'Now wait a minute, Balor, we know that you have remarkable powers of regeneration, but your claim is —'

'Fantastic, Doctor?' Balor met her eyes. 'I assure you that I do not exaggerate. And I am fully aware of the implication of my statement. If a thing is indestructible it will last forever. I am immortal.'

He had their attention and he held it, his voice quietening a little as he continued.

'It was no accident of evolution which made me what I am. Like many of your number I am a scientist. In happier times on my world I studied the complex nature of cell composition; the essence

111

of the vital life forces, the effects of controlled radiation on the nucleonic acids, the temporal interchange of sub-atomic particles. Our techniques and knowledge were great, but even so it took many years. Suffice to say that I succeeded. I learned how to eliminate the ageing process from living tissue, to achieve regeneration and to accelerate the healing process and to compress full basic knowledge of the overall pattern into each and every cell. Do you understand?'

Bergman nodded. 'Yes. So you learned these new techniques and you, naturally, applied them to yourself. Then—'

'Not only to myself, Professor!' Balor's tone was sharp. 'I gave the secret to my people and to my world. Death was defeated together with disease. Cripples became a relic of the past and life, to each, became an eternity of joy. Centuries passed and then a terrible malaise began to affect my people. They grew bored. Instead of devoting themselves to the pursuit of science and the search for knowledge they amused themselves with irrational pastimes—battles, wars, conflicts, strife of all kind, struggles which were futile because no one could be hurt and no one could die. A madness which I had not foreseen.'

'Children,' said Helena, quietly. 'Did the treatment give sterility?'

'Yes—and you have guessed the reason for the malaise and the hate which followed it. A hate directed against myself. The process of immortality could not be reversed and, when I admitted final defeat, they turned against me. A prison was built from adamantine materials and I was sealed in it

112

and sent into space to wander for eternity. Can you begin to imagine the torment I suffered?'

'A terrible punishment,' said Helena sympathetically. 'I can understand your people's regret at having lost the ability to bear children, but to do that to a living, thinking man!'

'I bear them no hatred. Time heals all wounds and a child must not be blamed for what it is. The power which guides the destiny of us all has saved me. You found me and released me from my prison. For that I am grateful. Grant me sanctuary and, in return, I will share my secrets with you.' Balor paused, looking from one to the other, 'You, Doctor! You, Professor! You, Commander! All of you—all will be as immortal as myself!'

The cabin was like a museum, shelves littered with model aircraft, early spaceships, replicas of various types of Eagles. An airship swung on a thread, a flimsy construction of paper and bamboo that was a memory of the first heavier-than-air machine to leave the ground, a painted aerial fighter that made a livid splotch of colour.

Baxter's world and his life.

He turned as a knock came from his door, opening the panel and staring at the tall figure of the alien. Balor smiled.

'May I enter?'

'Why not?' The pilot gestured to a chair. 'Help yourself.'

'No, my friend, I have come to help you, not myself. You take your flying very seriously, am I correct?'

'You are.'

'And I understand that some minor physical

disability has proved to be something of an inconvenience, yes?'

Baxter looked at his hands. They were clenched, the knuckles white. He said, tensely, 'If you've come here to mock me then get the hell out!'

'Mock?' The alien shook his head. 'I offer you my help. I am a stranger, needing friends, and you could be one. If I heal your eyes—'

'Mister, you do that and I'm yours for life. But if you're kidding me—'

'Relax, my friend. Trust me.' Balor raised his hands and moved towards where the pilot stood, palms outward, thumbs lifted to touch the other man's closed eyes. 'It will only take a moment,' he said quietly. 'A simple adjustment and all will be well.' His face changed, became suddenly gloating, an expression which Baxter was unable to see.

An expression which vanished as Koenig entered the room.

'What's going on here?'

'I am helping your companion.' Balor dropped his hands. 'There, it is done. And now, if you will excuse me?'

Baxter shook his head as the door closed behind the alien. His eyes, now open, looked dazed.

'My head,' he muttered. 'There's something—is that you, Commander?'

'Yes. What was Balor doing in here?'

'He came to help me. He promised to fix my eyes. My eyes!' Baxter's hand lifted, hovered inches from his distended pupils. 'I can't—you bastard! You lying bastard! I'll kill you for that!'

Models crashed as he turned, wood splintering, paper shredding, plastic shattering into jagged fragments. A slender cone of polished metal, the prototype of an early rocket ship, lay close and Baxter grabbed it, slashing with it, using it like a club.

A blow sent Koenig staggering back with blood streaming from his temple.

'Mike, for God's sake, what's wrong with you?'

Baxter snarled, moving in, the model a swinging weight in his hand. Koenig dodged, felt his feet hit something which rolled, fell as the club slammed against his jaw.

Baxter kicked, the toe of his boot driving against a rib, a knee, the point of the jaw. Desperately Koenig grabbed at his commlock, activated it as again the boot lifted.

'Help! Baxter's cabin! Come immediately!'

Then the boot landed and Koenig fell into darkness.

He awoke to stare at Balor's calmly smiling face.

'It seems I returned in good time, Commander.'

'Baxter?'

'Is unfortunately dead. Now, can you rise?'

Koenig felt the grip of the hand, the tremendous strength which lifted him with effortless ease. Wonderingly he touched his face, his jaw. It had been battered, the bone splintered, the nose broken, the skin torn and bruised. A boot had broken a rib —but there was no pain. He had been clubbed almost to death—but there were no marks.

'You healed me,' he said. 'It had to be you.'

'A small return, Commander, for you having released me from my prison.'

'And Baxter?' Koenig frowned, remembering. 'You did something to him. Promised to restore his eyes, but something went wrong.'

'No, nothing went wrong, Commander.'

'But he couldn't recognize me. He thought that I was you. He tried to kill me.'

'And almost succeeded,' said Balor calmly. 'A most amusing episode. It is gratifying to know that your race can be manipulated so easily. The expenditure of one unit can be replaced later when I set up the breeding programme. From what I have learned your species multiplies very rapidly. That, too, is gratifying to learn.'

Koenig said, flatly, 'What the hell are you talking about?'

'Isn't it clear? You disappoint me, Commander. I had considered you to be a person of sharp intelligence. I am taking over your little world. You will remain in nominal control, but you will take your orders from me. Any reluctance to obey will result in immediate punishment.' Balor threw open the cabin door. Outside, in the passage, lay the slumped figures of three security men—the guards who had answered the appeal for help.

'They aren't dead,' said Balor casually, 'but I have no inclination to heal their injuries. Your own doctors can do that while I—'

'You're mad,' said Koenig. 'Insane!'

Balor snarled, his hands reaching out, gripping, lifting as they tightened. Koenig swung, choking, tearing at the fingers clamped around his throat. A moment before he lost consciousness he was slammed down on his feet.

'I will not kill you, Commander, that would be too easy for you. But if you annoy me again I will break certain bones and rupture certain organs. You will live on as a cripple and I shall gain pleasure from watching you. But you will not die, John Koenig—I will make sure of that!'

Bergman, said, bleakly, 'A psychopath. A madman. Well, now we know.'

'The paintings,' said Helena. 'They were put in the ovoid to remind him of why he had been punished. John, he must be a monster! Why didn't they kill him?'

'They couldn't,' said Koenig. 'He's immortal.'

A creature who could not be killed, trapped and confined by a race who could do nothing but hurl him into space away from all human contact. Like a disease they had isolated, but could not destroy. An evil entity now released and raging through the base.

Kane called from the computer. 'Lower section monitors destroyed, Commander. Alien now heading towards power junctions F and G.'

'Continue monitoring progress.'

Balor was running wild, destroying, forcing the personnel to accept him as their ruler. Three men lay in the Medical Centre, seven more nursed their bruises, two women lay unconscious, their uniforms smeared with blood.

The helpless victims of an alien's sadistic greed for the sight of pain, object lessons to bring the base to its knees.

Morrow said, from where he sat at his console, 'He's heading towards sector 9. How about if we set up a party with lasers to cut him into pieces?'

'No.' Lasers had been tried—the beams had burned but the alien had healed and those who used the weapons had suffered. 'We can't risk it, Paul. He's about ready to tear the place apart. If he should decide to trigger the piles it'll be curtains.'

'But we've got to do something!'

'We will, but we've got to wait until Balor heads in the right direction.' Koenig looked at the illuminated plan of the base spread on a table next to the console. 'Here!' His finger tapped a point. 'I'm going down now to make ready. Keep alert. We're only going to get one chance so don't waste it.'

'Commander—'

'You heard what I said,' snapped Koenig. 'When he's in the right place hit the button. That's all you have to think about. Just hit it when he's set and never mind anything else.'

An order which might send him to his death, but one which had to be given. Koenig dismissed it from his mind as he moved down towards the lower levels and along a passage leading to an emergency air-lock. It took only a moment to remove the identifying symbols. To a stranger, an alien, the open door and the vestibule with the outer door closed would look like any other part of the complex.

How to kill an immortal?

It couldn't be done.

How to get rid of him?

The answer lay beyond the door at the end of the vestibule.

'Commander—here he comes!'

The voice from the commlock was thin, tense with excitement, a tension which Koenig shared. He stepped forward as Balor came into view along the passage.

'Master!'

'What?' A smile broke the cold hostility of the

handsome features. 'You acknowledge me, that is well. I think we shall work in harmony, my friend. But what made you change your mind? The destruction? The little interludes of pleasure in which I have indulged? A pity your bodies are so soft and fragile, but that may be remedied one day. Well?'

Koenig said, 'Among your people were you—unusual? Did you have senses and feelings which others regarded as vile? I ask only because I want to understand. If that was so then you will know why I am eager to help you.'

'A kindred spirit?' Balor's eyes flickered. 'Can it be possible?'

'Baxter had a hobby,' said Koenig quickly. 'You saw his models. I also have a hobby. Paintings which may interest you. I keep them in a secluded compartment beyond that door.' He moved casually towards the vestibule. 'If you would care to see them I would be honoured.'

An invitation which he hoped the alien, bored, curious and contemptuous of the prowess of his inferiors, would readily accept.

Balor halted on the edge of the vestibule.

'Beyond that door?'

'Yes, Master.' Koenig was already inside. He turned, smiling, extending his hand. 'Will you follow me?'

'*I* follow *you?*' Balor's smile held contempt. 'You forget your place, Commander. It is I who lead.'

He stepped forward into the chamber.

Koenig dived back towards the door, hit the jamb, fell and rolled as he yelled.

'Now, damn you! Now!'

Already they had hesitated too long, giving him

a chance despite his orders. But the button had been pressed and the inner door closed even as the alien turned, recognizing his danger a fraction too late. Koenig had a glimpse of his face as the panel slammed, the eyes flaring, the mouth parted in a snarl—then it was over.

The outer door opened, air gusted out, expanding as it carried itself and the contents of the vestibule into the void.

Sending the body of the alien spinning high and far, to vanish into the dark immensities of space.

CHAPTER ELEVEN

John Koenig woke from a dream in which he was falling through a vast emptiness and looked at the ceiling of his cabin, saw the minute flecks and cracks it contained, the signs of wear and strain which affected the entire base and was reflected to some extent in the personnel. Now, small irritations grew large too quickly, tempers were short, answers, at times, were curt.

Tension held and maintained too long would cause such symptoms. Hope which had begun to fade would make its contribution to the general lowering of morale.

Rising to wash and dress Koenig decided that changes would have to be made. Duties could be rotated on a wider basis and some new sports could be devised with teams picked to create a harmless spirit of rivalry. There could be more socializing and new areas could be fashioned to offer extended recreational facilities. Life was not all work and food and endless dedication. Fun had its place and so did romance.

And, he thought later as he sat in the dining area, something needed to be done about the food.

Emil Kranz shrugged when Koenig mentioned it.

'We can't perform miracles, John. To get sugar we've got to provide facilities to grow beets, which means we have to cut down on cereals. And we need sugar to feed the yeast which provides the basic materials for surrogate milk, bread, butter, compotes of fruit, meat and scrambled eggs. The algae is more economical, but that needs plenty of light, which means a larger share of power, which means less for—'

'I know, Emil,' said Koenig. 'But we're not short of power.'

'—digging new caverns, crushing stone and treating it so that it becomes soil, sterilizing the working areas and converting lunar deposits into water and useful chemicals.' Kranz paused for breath. 'And power alone isn't enough, Commander. We also need manpower. We still haven't got a surplus of labour over and above that needed for essential maintenance. Do you realize how many man-hours it takes to develop a new strain of yeast, to flavour it, gain the correct consistency appropriate to, say, steak or fish, and then to get it into full-scale production?'

'Too many,' said Koenig. 'And it always takes too long. I'm not grumbling, Emil, just requesting.

That coffee was pretty grim and the butter had a tang which reminded me of old boots.'

'A bad batch,' admitted Kranz. 'A strain became contaminated and we had either to use it or restrict the menu to basic pabulum. I figured that the personnel would rather have food which looked familiar than live on porridge for a few weeks. But don't worry about the taste, we've developed a salt which will take care of that. Kranz hesitated. 'Any chance of us striking it lucky soon, John?'

Koenig was honest. 'I doubt it, Emil, but we can always hope.'

Hope which was far from strong, as, later, he looked at the screens in Main Mission. The planet they depicted shone like a ball of polished ice which, as the sensors reported, was practically what it was. A frozen orb of snow and ice and frigid cold. A bleak world set far from its sun and turning endlessly in space; the last chance they would have of finding a habitable place before they left this solar system and went journeying again among the stars.

'Paul?'

'Nothing, Commander,' said Morrow from his console. 'I've covered all bands but can only get a blur of static.'

'Sandra?'

'Surface temperature is hard to get because of the shielding layer of mist, but I'm getting extremes of twenty below freezing during the day and up to a hundred lower during the night. If anyone wants a deep-freeze planet, this is it.'

Confirmation of what he already knew, but life was stubborn and so was hope. Kano did little to encourage it.

'Theoretically, Commander, life could exist under

those conditions, but its metabolism would be slow and the construction vegetative by nature. Simple lichens, some fungi, small herbivores.'

'We have penguins in the Antarctic, David. Does the computer know that?'

A feeble joke—the computer knew everything known to the race which had built it. Kano did not smile.

'The circumstances are not the same, Commander. The climate for one thing and—'

'I know, David. Just put it down to my inability to accept fully the idea that a machine knows more than all of us put together.' Privately Koenig thought that, at times, Kano was getting too much like a machine himself. 'Well Paul, we may as well—' Koenig frowned as light flashed on the panel. 'What's the matter?'

'The automatic reception signal!' Morrow sent his hands flying over the switches. 'Commander, someone is trying to make contact!'

The voice was thin, blurred, the words torn by washes of static. But it was a human voice.

And it could be understood.

'Hello. Hello. Calling Earth's moon! Calling Alpha Moonbase. Can you read me? Reply if you can read me. Hello. Hello. Calling—'

As the voice dissolved in a blur of crackling and electronic noise Koenig said, sharply. 'Respond, Paul. And get a fix on that transmitter.'

'Am doing, Commander.' Morrow's voice rose as he spoke into a microphone. 'Calling Ice Planet. Alpha calling Ice Planet. Maintain contact! Keep transmitting!'

The voice again.

'. . . long life here, a long life which you could share if . . .'

Another voice, fainter but unmistakable.

'. . . lane and no turning. Lost and with no final end. Be warned and yield not to temptation. Suffer . . .'

'Shut up, Tanner!' The first voice sounded irate. 'You crazy fool, this is the only chance we may ever get. Hello, Alpha. Come and join us. Ultima Thule is a paradise. Come and share it.'

'Stay away! Stay away!'

The voices blurred, faded, became empty sounds without form or meaning. Morrow shook his head as he worked at the console.

'Nothing, Commander.'

'There was a sudden eddy of mist just about then,' reported Sandra. 'It is highly charged and could be creating the static. They must have beamed through a temporary gap which has now closed.' Pausing she added, wonderingly, 'Those were Earth people talking, Commander. They knew who we were. They invited us to join them—at least one did. The other warned us to stay away. But why should he do that? Surely they must want to be rescued.'

'We were asked to share in a paradise,' said Kano. He looked at the bleak world which they were passing. 'That? A paradise?'

It was the innermost hell of Dante's inferno, the seventh to which the most evil souls were sent to suffer the worst torments. A place of ice, not fire, of cold, not heat. Koenig studied it in the screens of the Eagle which carried him down.

At his side in the pilot's chair Carter said, 'It's

124

like flying into cotton wool. I've flown blind before and in some of the worst smog on record, but this is beyond a joke. Are they still transmitting?'

'Paul doesn't know,' said Koenig. 'But we assume they are. Not that it makes any difference, the computer plotted the source-point and is guiding us down towards it.'

'Which cheers me up no end,' said Carter. 'To be controlled every inch of the way by a machine back on Alpha. I don't have David's trust in that thing. It could make a mistake and, at a time like this, one would be one too many.'

He was talking to ease his nerves, Koenig knew, a little irritable at not being in full control, and he could sympathize with the pilot. Leaning forward he checked the flight-instruments but they told him nothing. Back in the passenger compartment Helena and Bergman would have more information from their on-board sensors.

In answer to his question Bergman said, 'We're mostly getting verification, John. There's a storm blowing down there, but we should land well to one side of the main force. The atmosphere is breathable and has a high percentage of oxygen which would be favourable to the support of any native life form. We've also spotted wide bands of temperature variation which are sweeping around the planet at a fairly high level. The variation is quite marked and it's almost as if heated jet-currents were orbiting the planet.'

'Heated?'

'An analogy,' said Bergman. 'They are simply much warmer in relation to the rest of the atmosphere. The temperature differential would lead to the generation of violent winds and the thick mist we have observed. It could also account for the tremendously high electronic noise we are picking up. Clear radio transmission can probably be made during periods of atmospheric tranquillity.'

'Which means that we are already cut off from contact with the base,' said Helena. 'We're operating on the flight extrapolations fed into the ship computer memory banks by the main instrument on Alpha.'

'Time of landing?'

'Ten minutes plus or minus two.'

It was plus and the landing was a hard one. Carter grunted as he released his safety harness.

'How far was it out, Commander?'

'Very little.' Koenig glanced at the instrument in his hands. 'The signal-source lies due west of here at a distance of approximately half a mile. To try and get closer in the Eagle could be to waste time. The reading is only an extrapolation and we could wind up further away than we are now. We'll have to walk.'

'In this?' Carter glanced at the screens which depicted the scene outside. Mist rolled like thick smoke over a plain of rugged ice.

'We'll wear survival gear and carry packs. The commlocks will guide us back to the Eagle if we should get separated—but we must make sure that doesn't happen.' Koenig put aside the locator as he began to slip into his suit.

Outside the cold struck like a knife. Within minutes, despite the protective clothing, they were numbed, breath pluming from ice-covered mouths, eyes stinging, feet and hands devoid of feeling. The mist pressed around them, stronger, colder, the wind rising as they forced their way over an expanse of broken, cracked and ice-bound terrain.

'The storm,' gasped Bergman. 'It must have shifted and is now heading towards us. Are we almost there, John?'

Koenig looked at the locator, holding it close and narrowing his eyes. The needles spun, settled, spun again as he triggered the mechanism.

'We're almost on top of the signal-source, assuming that the computer extrapolated correctly.'

'And that the local interference isn't affecting the pathfinder,' said Carter. 'If the transmitter is here why can't we see it?'

'It could be underground,' suggested Helena. 'Or over that way—or that.' She stared helplessly at the mist which cut visibility to inches.

Koenig lifted his commlock. 'Hello. Hello. If anyone can receive me please answer.' He repeated the call and waited, holding the instrument close to his ear against the hum and wail of the strengthening wind.

The answer, when it came, was the distant cry of a ghost.

'Men of Alpha do you hear me? Have you arrived yet? Why do you not . . .'

Static roared and drowned the thin voice. Irritably Koenig shook his head.

'They know we are here, but standing around like this isn't getting us anywhere. The best thing would be to return to the ship, rig up a visual signal and let them find us.' He triggered the commlock and heard the homing signal. 'You all receiving? Good. Let's move!'

Three minutes later the locator signals died, the sound drowned by a gusting roar of static which heralded a blast of wind which tore them from their feet and sent them rolling over the ice like fallen ninepins.

A blast which sent mist swirling, thickening, closing in like an opaque curtain.

When Koenig finally managed to struggle to his feet he was alone.

The commlock gave only a susuration of formless sound, a directionless noise which meant nothing. Far overhead one of the relatively warm currents must be passing and causing the ether to become an electronic cacophony. Even so he tried, calling the others one after the other, ceasing only when it became obvious he was wasting his time.

Shouting came next.

'Helena! Alan! Victor!'

The mist caught the sound, reflected it, muffled even the echoes so that it was like shouting against an enveloping woollen blanket.

Alone and lost Koenig forced himself to be calm.

He could sit and wait for the electronic storm to pass and the locator to work again, but if he did that he would freeze. He could move around to gain some body-heat from exertion, but if he did that he would quickly tire and fall a victim to hypothermia. A bitter choice with death waiting no matter which path he chose if he failed to find the Eagle in time.

'John! John!'

A voice an inch away or a mile? It came again and Koenig yelled back, listening, shouting again as he moved into the mist. Two steps and he saw the loom of something dark. Two more and Bergman stood before him.

'John! Thank God I found you! Have you seen the others?'

'No.' Koenig tore at his equipment and loosened a long strap. He joined it to another he took from Bergman's pack, tied one end of the make-shift rope to the other's belt, the remaining end to his own. 'Move out until this is taut between us, then keep moving until you've covered a circle.'

The rope wasn't long enough, the area covered too small. Teeth chattering from his forced inactivity Koenig lengthened the rope with fabric ripped from his clothing, gaining a few precious feet. He took twenty steps to his right.

'Right, Victor. Do it again.'

'You should be moving, John, if you don't you'll freeze.

'Hurry!'

Helena could be out there, inches away, a foot at the most and yet as invisible as if she'd been on another world. Alan too, wandering, stumbling, perhaps, hands outstretched as if he were blind.

He *was* blind.

They were all blind.

An object a foot away beyond visual reach and a gust of wind could have blown them together now and Koenig felt he had used his entire quota in finding Bergman.

He pulled at the rope and the professor came towards him shaking his head.

'Nothing, John. Perhaps if we spread out and both walked in the same direction we'd have better luck.'

A narrow search-path cut through the fog and the chance of it finding anyone was remote. But it would keep them both moving and anything was better than making no attempt at all.

Koenig lifted his commlock, listened to the wash

of static, then took a chance. His sense of direction was completely disturbed and he had no idea as to where the ship could be, but the direction he was facing could be as right as any other.

'Move to the end of the line, Victor. We'll walk a hundred steps then see how things are. Keep them short, neither of us wants to risk a fall and a broken bone.'

'We could make a rough camp, John. We have solid fuel burners in the packs and some food. A fire could serve as a beacon.'

'We'll see. A fire would stand more chance of being spotted at night. Just walk and keep shouting and, remember, a hundred short steps.'

Koenig felt Bergman fall at the eighty-seventh.

The line jerked and went slack to tighten again with a snap which made him fear that it had been broken. Koenig traced it through the mist, followed it as it sloped down and touched the recumbent figure.

'Victor?'

Bergman was cold. Beneath the ice crusting his mouth his lips were blue and his eyes were glazed. Koenig rubbed at his cheeks, knowing that he was fighting a losing battle. Body-heat, lost, needed time to be regained. The wind sucked the warmth from their bodies and, despite their activity, hypothermia—extreme loss of natural warmth, would kill them.

'Victor!' Koenig's voice became harsh. 'Are you hurt? No? Then get up, man! Up!'

Bergman climbed shakily to his feet.

'A fire—'

The materials were held in a box; a few slugs of solid fuel, a burner, heat enough to cook a few meals in case of dire need. Koenig squatted, rasped the igniters over the rough plates, set down the fuel as it broke into flame.

The wind tore at the heat, dissipated it before it could give them its warmth.

'We must keep moving, Victor.' Koenig beat his arms across his chest and again tried the commlock. The static had lessened and, faintly, he could hear the signal beacon from the Eagle. Turning the instrument he found the direction in which the ship must be. 'Come on, Victor!'

Bergman stumbled after the first few steps and fell to lie gasping. His teeth chattered and it was hard for him to speak. His whole body quivered with an uncontrollable ague-like reaction to the cold.

'Leave me, John. Alone you might make it. I've got to rest, to get warm somehow, to sleep . . . sleep . . .'

'Up!' Koenig hauled the limp figure to its feet. 'Move, Victor! Damn you, move!'

He plunged into the mist, one arm supporting the elder man, feeling the shakes which told of hypothermia. Bergman was dying. In minutes he would be past the point where he could be revived.

Koenig checked his commlock, swore as static drowned out the signal. Blindly he pressed on, Bergman a dead weight now which hung over his shoulder. Death, invisible but present, kept him close company.

'Hello there! Hello! Answer if you can hear me. Hello!'

A voice incredibly near followed by bulky figures which loomed from the mist. Men which clustered around and formed a living wall against the wind.

'Are you from Alpha?'

'Yes.' Koenig peered at the cowled faces, blurred but unmistakably human. 'There are others—we became separated.'

'One has been found.' The deep voice boomed from the hood. 'There.'

Koenig stared at the almost shapeless bundle some of the men were carrying. It was Helena and she was unconscious, there were thick furs wrapped around her own garments.

'She was in a bad way when we found her,' boomed the voice. 'Like your friend here. We'd better get you all back to the palace.'

'There's another,' said Koenig. 'Alan Carter, our pilot.'

'We'll keep looking, but I'll be frank with you, his chances are small. Come on, now, let's get you to where there is warmth and protection from this damned wind.'

CHAPTER TWELVE

Helena stirred and opened her eyes and looked at a scene from one of the story books she had read when a very young girl before the cold disciplines of science had ousted the world of fantasy from her life. Above soared the dome of a cavern each fragment covered in glittering crystals, the facets reflecting a rainbow pattern of lights in scintillating brilliance.

More light pulsed from a point below her vision and she lifted her head and saw a great mass of redly glowing crystals lying heaped within a circle of others which shimmered with blues and greens, lambent yellow and smokey violet.

'Helena!' Turning she looked at Koenig, saw the anxiety in his eyes, the sudden relief as she moved and smiled. 'Thank God you've recovered!'

'The others?'

'Victor is here with us.' Koenig gestured to where Bergman lay close to the fire on a heap of furs. 'Alan is still missing. They're looking for him, but the chance of finding him alive is negligible.'

She remembered the wind, the mist, the numbing cold and, finally, the shapes which had suddenly appeared as if from delirium. The last thing she remembered.

Sitting upright she looked around. The cavern was vast, the walls pierced with openings which, she guessed, led to interconnecting chambers. Men and women sat or sprawled around the strangely glowing fire, all dressed in a variety of skins and furs. More furs lay in scattered piles to form beds. Articles of furniture stood around; tables and benches made of stone, chairs fashioned of metal and plastic.

Space ship furniture of a pattern she knew.

'John, who are these people?'

'Survivors, Helena. They call this planet Ultima Thule. Do you remember the Uranus expedition of 1986?'

'Naturally, but the entire expedition was totally destroyed in a proton storm five days from their objective.' Helena stared at him with startled understanding. 'Are you saying that these people are the survivors? John, that's incredible!'

'Incredible, but true.' The deep voice boomed from the massive chest of a man who came towards them. He wore furs as if they had been cloth of gold adorned with purple. He carried a cup which steamed and yielded a pleasing fragrance. 'As your own eyes should tell you, Doctor Russell.'

'Doctor Rowland! Cabot!'

'The same.' Rowland bowed as he handed her the cup. 'Try this tisane which I made from the contents of your pack. The years have improved you, Helena. As I remember you were a little too thin and far too serious. You needed a husband or a lover to teach you how to enjoy life. Now, I assume, you have both.'

'I had both,' she corrected. 'My husband died years ago.'

'And now it's time for another, perhaps?' He glanced at Koenig. 'Well, time for reminiscing later on, now drink and relax. You've had a hard time.'

'Hard,' said a new voice. 'Hard? Is a conundrum hard to crack? Is an egg? Read me the riddle of the spheres, my pretty, and I will twine stars in your hair for a crown.'

The voice was high, thin, the man a parody. If Rowland was a king the other was a jester. His fur boots were pointed at the toes, his fur cap cut like that of a fool, his robe slashed and tattered, ragged ends flying as he spun and danced. His eyes were small, shrewd and darting. His face, at times vacuous, at others creased in the wizened likeness of an ape.

134

As Helena stared at him he began to dance and sing an air she vaguely remembered.

'Hey de, hey de! Misery me, lackaday de. He sipped no sup and he craved no crumb as he sighed for the love of a lady.'

The Gilbert and Sullivan theme from the *Yeoman of the Guard.*

Rowland boomed, 'Shut up, Jack. Come and be introduced properly. Doctor Helena Russell meet Colonel Jack Tanner, Commander of the Uranus Expeditionary probe.'

'Call me Jack,' said Tanner quickly before Helena could say anything. 'Call me Jack—for I am Jack the Fool. And in folly I am not alone, for see? The other of your number wakes and stares with eyes which need the light of suns to show the answers he seeks.' He danced to where Bergman had sat upright on the heap of furs. 'I'll bet we are in this land of dreams where nothing is but as it seems.'

'Colonel Tanner!' Bergman stared his amazement. 'And Doctor Rowland!'

'We are not ghosts,' said Tanner. 'Though we wander and howl bitterly into the night. But heed my warning, eat nothing which you have not brought with you. Only the water will prove gentle to your taste.'

'Professor Bergman, your arrival here has made this the happiest day of my life,' said Rowland. 'There is so much to explain, to talk about. Discoveries with tremendous implications and—'

'Why did the Colonel warn us against the food?'

'It takes a little getting used to. When we first arrived it made us all violently ill, but we adapted in time.'

Bergman nodded then said, 'But how did you

135

get here? The last we heard of the Uranus expedition was that your ship was breaking up in a proton storm. That was about fourteen years ago now.'

'I made the report,' said Tanner. 'Once upon a time I spoke simple truth. Time had riddled it a little but it is as it was—true.'

'We were lucky,' said Rowland grimly. 'And something odd happened. The ship went out of control and for a while we were helpless. The instruments gave incredible readings, we had run out of prayers, and all hell had broken loose within the hull. Maybe one of those prayers was answered or perhaps we hit a nexus of opposed forces just when the pile burst and ran wild. We should all have been killed with the wild radiation let alone the heat, but it was a time for miracles. Something happened. A movement in a plane other than the normal three. My guess is that we were nipped in opposed forces like a cherry stone between finger and thumb. When they pressed we were shot somewhere.'

'A space warp,' said Bergman thoughtfully. 'If the forces were strong enough and correctly opposed and you were in the nexus then you would have been rotated into the fourth dimension. Your own power source would have kept you there for an indeterminate period and then, as it waned, you would have reverted back into normal time and space.'

'Not normal, Professor. You can't call this universe we're in normal.'

'Not as we usually regard normality, no,' admitted Bergman. 'But normal in relation to the fourth-dimensional plane into which you must have been thrown. And then?'

'We broke out or whatever you like to call it. We managed to repair the ship enough to make a landing and we came here.' Rowland gestured at the cavern. 'We managed to survive and—' He turned as a party of fur-clad men came through an opening and wended their way down a ramp towards the fire. 'Well? Did you find him, Ted?'

'No.' The man was shivering. 'It's dark out there now and nothing living could survive. I'm sorry, folks, but there it is. Your friend has to be dead.'

Mathematicians had once said that a bee couldn't fly, that acceleration pressure would kill anyone moving at more than fifteen miles an hour, that men would never traverse space. They had been experts and had been shown to be wrong.

Ted was an expert and Carter made him a liar. The pilot was still alive.

He crawled over crusted snow and polished ice, hands extended as he pushed on through the mist and darkness, a living thing driven on by the determination to survive.

Logic had nothing to do with it. Logically his chances were so small as to be non-existent, and neither did sense, a sensible man would have stopped and welcomed death as a friend. Frozen, numbed, dying, Carter fought on, knowing only that to halt was to die, that to keep on moving would be to maintian life a few minutes longer, an extension bought with pain.

Pain which multiplied as his head slammed against something hard.

An ice-covered rock barred his progress and he

touched it, moving along it, ankles and knees scraping over the ground. His hands were like wood and told him nothing aside from the fact that he had met a barrier. But there had been no barrier on the way from the Eagle to the location point. Lost, he had wandered in the wrong direction and he had no more strength.

All he could do was to lie against the mound and hope that it would break the force of the wind.

Blearily he stared at the commlock in his hand. The screen was dark but the instrument emitted a regular bleeping sound. The location signal from the Eagle, coming through during a patch of calm. He turned the instrument, frowning as the signal did not vary. It took several moments for him to realize why it stayed the same.

He had found the Eagle! The mount against which he lay had to be the bulk of the vessel itself!

Hope brought him to his feet, the commlock extended pointing at the place where the air-lock should be. Unless the electronic device worked he was dead—his numbed hands could never operate the manual combination lock. Again he clamped his hand on the commlock activating stud and moved it from side to side.

'Work! Please work! Dear God, make it work!'

He was praying, trembling, knowing that safety lay only inches away, but unless the lock opened it could have been on another world.

A stir in the snow covering the bulk, a splinter of light which grew into an oblong, a gust of relative heat which sent thick streamers of mist to join the other fog all around.

Carter stumbled forward, reached for the edge

of the port and was suddenly smashed aside by something big and shaggy.

A beast, as high as his waist, thick with ice-crusted wool, long horns sweeping forward over savage eyes filmed with nictating lids.

The face was long and narrow, the jaw pointed, the lips thin over flat teeth. A creature native to this world, adapted to the bitter climate, attracted by the heat of his body, the nourishment it contained.

A killer.

It came with a rush, a horn catching at Carter's clothing, ripping it and the flesh beneath so that blood dappled the snow. An attack which would have ripped him open had he not lunged to one side just in time. A lunge which left him sprawling helplessly on the ice, rolling as razor-sharp hooves sent splinters into his face.

Desperately he grabbed at his belt. The laser was gone but he'd opened his pack and wrapped what it contained around himself, stuffing the food and fuel into his pockets. As the beast charged again Carter snatched out a lump of solid fuel, gripped it in his teeth and slashed the end over the igniter.

Flame stung his eyes and crisped his eyebrows, growing as he snatched the fragment from his mouth and threw it directly into the gaping jaws of the attacking beast.

As the thing reared, bellowing, Carter threw himself into the air-lock and slapped his hand against the button triggering the cycle. As the outer door closed he slumped, falling through the portal as the inner door opened to land sprawling on the floor of the Eagle, breath panting, eyes closed, blood forming a pool beneath him where it seeped from his wounded side.

From the panel came Morrow's voice, thin and anxious with rising urgency.

'Come in Eagle One. Do you copy? Come in Eagle One. If you hear me answer. Alpha calling Eagle One.'

Carter heaved himself to his feet and fell into the pilot's chair.

'Paul . . . can you hear me, Paul?'

'Alan! What's happening?'

'Trouble. We got separated in the storm. I was lucky to make it back. Found the Eagle by accident.'

'Alan are you hurt? Your voice—'

'Hurt,' said Carter. 'A beast nearly got me. It could have got the others if they survived the cold. You'll have to handle the Eagle, Paul. Can't stay conscious much longer.' Carter sagged, staring at the screen, the face which suddenly appeared.

At his console Morrow said, 'Dear God, look at him, David! Frostbitten, bleeding, he looks all in.'

'We've got to get him up while the electronic calm allows it,' said Kano. 'The computer says we could just have enough time if you start immediately.'

'But the others? John, Victor, Helena?'

'Nothing could live unprotected down there, Paul. The temperature's hit bottom. It's a miracle that Alan is still alive and he won't be for long unless you bring him up and soon. Do it, Paul. Save one of them at least.'

A moment then Morrow nodded. Lolling in the pilot's chair Carter didn't see the panel flare to life or hear the pulse of the engines as they fed power

140

into the drive. Couldn't tell when the Eagle lifted to start the journey back to base.

The journey which alone could save his life.

Bergman was entranced. He said, 'Do you mean that you built all this equipment from material salvaged from the Uranus probe? It seems incredible.' He glanced at the grotto-like chamber crammed with electronic and other devices, recognizing some of the instruments, frowning at others. At his side Ted Foster, the engineer of the Uranus expedition, beamed his pride.

'We had to do a lot of improvisation, Professor, and stretch what we had. Some of the crystals yield a rare element when fused and we found a vein of heavy metal. Our biggest initial trouble was the food.'

'You couldn't eat it,' said Bergman. 'But how did you manage to adapt?'

'The hard way.' Foster was grim. 'Rowland will want to tell you that himself, but aside from the food the early days were tough. If we hadn't found this place we'd never have made it.'

'But you did.'

'Yes, we went Robinson Crusoe one better.' Foster watched as Bergman examined a case. It contained vegetables growing in a bed of snow. 'Thulian salad.'

'It looks appetizing enough.'

'Looks can deceive. It has a harsh, bitter taste which we're trying to breed out, but in its natural state it provides the sample diet for a species of animal which roams the surface. It grows beneath the snow and they can scent it out.'

'Animals?'

'Things like big sheep with long horns like those of an ox.' Foster hesitated. 'They are pretty vicious and take a lot of killing. They come out at dusk.'

Bergman knew he was thinking of Carter, but said nothing, the search parties had done their best and it would be wrong to complain especially as they owed their lives to the Thulians.

Instead, looking around, he said, 'You've done wonders, Ted.'

Tanner came prancing forward. 'Of wonder! Science in the belly and salad on the brain.'

The man was deranged, he had to be, and Bergman wondered why he had the run of the place. Surely he held a potential danger in his wild caperings and mindless babbling. Perhaps a previous respect still held sway; he had, after all, been the Commander.

Glancing at two tall transparent cabinets he said, to Foster. 'Tell me something of these, Ted.'

Tanner gave the other no chance to reply.

'Toys for the professor,' he chuckled. 'New toys to play with time. Take care! They'll twist you out of mind!'

Like a child he cavorted towards the crystal fire in the main cavern, halting to stand beside Helena where she lay sleeping. Bending down he whispered in her ear.

'Go home!' Again, in her other ear. 'Go home!'

'What?' She woke and stared at him. 'Colonel?'

'Go home to Alpha!'

Helena rose as he danced away. Frieda, Foster's woman, stood with some other Thulians watching her. As if coming to a sudden decision she approached, took Helena by the hand and led her close to the strange fire.

'He's right, Doctor. Go home to Alpha.'

'Why?'

'Doom sits on a pinnacle of ice and no birds sing.'

Frieda ignored Tanner's interruption. 'You must not stay here. There is nothing here for you. We are living people frozen in eternity. You must go home to Alpha.'

'But Alpha isn't home,' said Helena. 'It's just a barracks on a mobile rock flying endlessly through space. We want a real home, a place to settle and to build. To form a new life and to have children—'

'There can be no children here!'

The harsh bleakness of the woman's voice was disconcerting. Helena said, 'But you asked us to come. We were invited by Doctor Rowland.'

'Ah, yes, the Doctor!' Tanner had crept towards her and was abruptly squatting at her side. 'But has he told you everything? Of the expedition, yes, of the storm and why we had to land on Ultima Thule and some of what we had to do in order to survive. But he hasn't told you yet that here we live forever, that we have been here for eight hundred and eighty years, that we haven't aged since we landed, that we are the same yesterday, today, tomorrow and that the price of immortality is impotence. No growth, no future, no end. Just ever and a day—' His arms flew wide in a gesture which embraced the watchers, the cavern, the planet itself. '—this!'

Rowland said, easily, 'Jack is inclined to dramatize everything. He exaggerates as you have probably noticed and he is, well, a little abnormal in certain ways. He mustn't be blamed for that. In many ways he is a hero.'

'I'm not denying that,' said Koenig. 'But is what he said true?' He had heard it from Helena and now they with Bergman faced Rowland in the communications room of the palace. A room which held the old ship computer now bulky with additional banks.

'It is true,' admitted Bergman. 'The age part, at least.'

'Victor?'

Bergman had been busy at the computer. He turned with a print-out in his hand, his face puzzled.

'It seems true enough, John. The year is 2870 —either they or we have been through some kind of time warp. They could have been thrown back while we could have been thrown forward. It isn't important just which, the result is the same. These people have lived close to nine hundred years on this world.'

Rowland said, 'Commander Koenig, I need your help. When we first landed here our concern was to survive. We had to adapt to the local conditions and it wasn't easy to take the necessary steps. We succeeded as you can see, but what we were losing, although we didn't know it, was our human biochemical structure. For centuries now I have tried to isolate the factor which has given us our longevity but always there has been one problem I cannot surmount.'

'You lacked a normal subject from which to obtain a comparison,' said Helena.

'Exactly, but that difficulty is now over. You are here, colleagues and fellow scientists, and together we will climb Olympus and wrest their secrets from the Gods. Listen to me and understand. The blight of human life has been death. The most brilliant minds cut off in their prime. Progress held back by accidents and the sheer inability of one man to live long enough to learn all there is to know in his field. But if we can leave Thule carrying with us the secret of longevity there will be no end—only better and more enticing beginnings. We shall find paradise!'

A dream as old as mankind itself. Never to grow old, to be always young, to learn, to see the future as something impossibly remote. To be given the time to harvest knowledge, to let it mature, to taste gracefully of life's pleasures.

To walk—not to run.

To linger—not to race past in a futile effort to extend the working span.

And the dream had bones of reality.

Koenig looked at what lay in a vast chamber and listened to the words of a man obsessed.

'We are rebuilding the Uranus probe but this time with improved engines. When we have the secret and when this ship is complete we shall own the universe. We shan't be dependent on your lumbering and uncontrollable moon. We shall travel wherever and whenever we please. But this is a matter of mere technology. I want you to join me now in one final experiment. Then together we will step forward into the greatest scientific adventure in the entire history of Man. Unencumbered by death we shall leap from planet to planet, star to star. We shall be gods!'

Gods—the word left a sour taste in Koenig's mouth. Once men forgot their humanity they turned into beasts not deities, animals not angels. Balor had been proof of that and here it was again, the same dream, the same promise, the same ambition—would the same decadence follow?

He felt a pull at his arm and heard Tanner's low whisper. 'I see a hungry mind. I'll feed it on wormwood and gall.'

'Meaning?'

Tanner grimaced and led Koenig from the chamber to a secluded cave in which glowed a crystal fire at which sat a group of men and women. They remained immobile, the ruby light shining on their glazed eyes, their vacuous faces.

'The Revered Ones,' said Tanner. 'The results of centuries of experiments. We take care of them, feed them, wash away their filth. They need nothing more and could do without that—what does a vegetable care about dirt?'

'Rowland?' Then, as Tanner nodded, Koenig said, 'Why didn't you stop him?'

'We were all scientists and we had to learn how to survive. As Commander I was the first to submit myself to the experiments. I was luckier than those you see. After a long time I regained what we wittily call my mind. It was a gamble I had to take —your people do not. Think of the woman, Commander, sitting here for centuries staring at nothing.

Tanner's voice broke, turned into a giggling laugh.

'Call me a fool if you will, gentle sir, but I'm not such a fool as that!'

CHAPTER THIRTEEN

Koenig burst into the laboratory just in time. Helena and Bergman were already in the transparent cabinets and Rowland had his hand on a panel of switches. He turned, frowning as Koenig tore open the cabinets and pulled the others from them.

'Commander! What are you doing!'

'Preventing what could be a mistake. Helena, Victor, did you know that they have a cave here in which idiots are kept? Poor devils whose minds have been ruined by experiments?'

Rowland said, sharply, 'They are volunteers. They understood the risks involved and accepted them.'

'Victor?'

'Doctor Rowland described the projected experiment as a development of epsilon ray analysis,' said Bergman. 'I respected his medical reputation on Earth and I admire his spectacular achievements here on Thule. I accepted his assurance that I would be in no danger.'

'Helena?'

'John, this is the greatest medical challenge we can face. The conquest of death is the implicit basis of the Hippocratic oath.'

'So you both intend to continue?'

'Why not, John?' Bergman was puzzled. 'What

harm can there be in a simple in-depth cellular analysis? Surely you have no suspicions of Doctor Rowland? What can he possibly hope to gain?'

'New recruits,' said Koenig bluntly. 'New followers and new workers for his project. But I can't stop you doing what you want. All I ask is that you delay for a while. Wait until after we've contacted Alpha. It won't be long. In a few days we must decide whether to evacuate or not.'

'I'm sorry,' said Rowland. 'We can't contact Alpha. Something is wrong with our communications equipment.'

'It doesn't matter. We still have the Eagle.'

'It has gone.' Rowland shrugged as he met their eyes. 'I would have told you. Search parties have failed to discover it.'

'John, Alan must have made it!' Helena stared at him, her eyes glowing. 'He's alive!'

'But he must think we're not.' Bergman frowned, thinking. 'Logic would dictate that as well as experience. Yet I can't believe they would abandon us without making another search. Doctor, are you sure your radio equipment can't be repaired?'

'My experiments! You can't fail me now! That analysis is essential if the secret of longevity is to be discovered!'

'No!' Frieda stood at the opening of the cavern, Tanner behind her, others clustered behind him. A schism in the group, Koenig guessed, and wondered just how much he had been used by the apparent madman and why. 'We don't need the secret. Mankind doesn't need it. We are cursed with it but we had no choice. I say that things have gone far enough.'

'Fool! What do you know about it?'

'I am a woman. I want children—where are they? We need to grow—how? Commander Koenig, do you want your people to become like we are? Is that the best you can hope to give them?'

Life, perhaps endless life, but with it would come stasis. And already he could see the problems. Who would refuse the gift in order to remain fertile, spending the years waiting, watching their youth slip away while others stayed unchanged? And if all took it what would be the point of existence at all? And, if none, would he ever dare to—No. It was unthinkable that such a gift could be ignored.

Taking Tanner to one side Koenig said, quietly, 'What's happening here, Jack?'

'A whistle in the dark, is that happening enough? Or does poor old Jack have to swing to show that he has a neck?'

'When Rowland begged us to come it was your voice which told us to stay away.'

'It had little effect, though you heard it well enough.' He sniffed suspiciously at the air. 'Strange, don't you think, that now they are so close your people should suffer your loss in silence?'

'Meaning what?'

'It's an ill wind that carries the stink of fish.'

And a nod was as good as a wink to a blind horse, thought Koenig sourly. The advantage of acting the fool was that anything you said could be taken two ways and innocence could always be claimed.

Rowland said, 'I'm sorry to press the point, Commander, but I would like to get on with my analysis. If you are ready, Professor? And you, Doctor?'

'I'd like to see those people in the cavern,' said

149

Helena abruptly. 'The ones who have lost their minds.'

'The Revered Ones? But certainly.' Rowland smiled. 'It may even be possible that you could give me your opinion on any hope of corrective therapy. If you will follow me, please? Frieda, isn't it time the meal was being prepared?'

For a moment the woman stood her ground and then, sullenly, turned and moved back into the main cavern, the others trooping after her.

As Rowland accompanied by Bergman and Helena left the chamber Koenig said, 'Right, Jack, now let's look at that communications equipment.'

It was a jumble of bits and pieces, circuits improvised, components substituted for others, the marks of genius and a wild inspiration mixed to produce an installation which would have any electronics engineer in a whirl.

Koenig probed as he traced and checked, pursing his lips as he snapped free a printed circuit which bore the marks of burning.

'Have you a replacement for this?'

'A replacement? No. But this should do the job as well.' Tanner passed over a complex component. 'You look at it oddly, and oddly you may look and, looking, the more oddly it appears the odder it seems.'

'Why?'

'A question to which there can be a multitude of answers,' crowed Tanner. 'Why this? Why that? Why therefore, why? Why not test the device and discover why it is like it is?'

'I wasn't talking about the radio.' Koenig clipped the part into place and stood, looking at his companion. 'Colonel Jack Tanner,' he said. 'Graduated

150

the top of his class, registered IQ of 176, three degrees and a mastery of inter-spacial mathematics
unequalled in the entire world. You weren't a fool
then and I don't believe you're one now.'

'Should I smile from under my arm to convince
you?'

'No. Is it because of Rowland?'

'Ask the Revered Ones.'

'Of whom you were once a member.' Koenig
pursed his lips. 'A bad time, but if you recovered
then why haven't the others? Perhaps you should
think of that.'

'And you should think of a moon. A moon and
a song in June to go with the moon. Ah, me, lackaday, Jack's dull today. Who wants a stupid fool?'

'King Rowland?' Koenig caught the flicker of
the eyes. 'God Rowland? God,' he repeated. 'A
man with such tremendous potential power. How to
control him? He isn't a basically bad man so why
shoot him? He is even a likeable man and was
once a close friend. And men who have faced death
together, who have travelled dimensions of unknown
space and have won through—such men share
something they can never lose. Respect, regard, even
a deep and abiding affection. Men who would die
for each other, who would kill—who might play a
part in order to maintain a sense of perspective.
Warm, Jack?'

'Too warm and you will burn.'

'A fool,' mused Koenig. 'In ancient times the
emperors used to hire men to ride in their chariots
behind them and to whisper in their ears, *You too
are mortal!* A reminder that they were not gods.
The fool of a king could make jests with impunity.
King Rowland,' he repeated. 'God Rowland. Jack

151

—you have my respect. The doctor is a lucky man to have a friend such as yourself.'

Tanner said, flatly, 'One thing straight. *I* am Thule's fool.'

'A job you can keep.' Koenig snapped a series of switches on the panel and paused with his hand on the final key. 'Here's hoping.'

Pressing the key he spoke.

'Koenig calling from Ultima Thule. Koenig calling Alpha. Do you read me? Answer if you receive me. Koenig calling Alpha base. Calling from Ultima Thule. Do you read me? Answer if you—'

Sound blasted from the speaker.

'Commander! Is that really you? You're alive and well?' Morrow's voice, strained, incredulous but reflecting his relief.

'Easy, Paul. Yes, we're all alive and well. Alan?'

'We got him back in time. He's a little stiff but otherwise OK. He's got a scratch or two but nothing to worry about. But the reception! Not a trace of static. Orders, Commander?'

'Send down an Eagle. Fix location on this signal and set up a guide programme in the ship computer. I'll try and arrange a homing signal. You'd better send—'

'No argument, Commander.' Carter's voice coming strong and clear and determined. 'I'm coming down in person.'

'No!' snapped Koenig. 'Alan, you're not fit enough. You can't!'

'He can't hear you,' said Morrow cheerfully. 'He's already on his way to the pad. Don't worry, I'll send Doctor Mathias down with him. Any chance of establishing visual contact?'

Koenig glanced at Tanner who shook his head.

'No. I'm using a special rig which must be draining the energy-source in order to blast a hole through the static by sheer power. Have you the location fixed? Good. Maintain contact with the Eagle.'

'A good name,' Tanner said as Koenig turned from the panel. 'A bird of prey sweeping down through the mist and cold to pick clean our bones. Yet, perhaps, this prey also has claws. What will be the outcome, Commander? Will we go or will you come? Shall we share your world or will you share ours?'

He twisted, cavorting, furs flapping, and Koenig could almost hear the jangle of bells.

'Well? Is the decision so hard to make, John Koenig? A plague on both your houses! Which is it to be?'

Mathias was entranced. He walked over the floor of the main cavern and halted before the crystal fire, holding out his hands as if to a brazier.

'Fantastic! A short radioactive half-life, I assume, but surely there must be attendant danger from emitted particles?'

'Very little.' Ted Foster was at his side. 'It's a peculiarity of these crystals that they generate a magnetic field under stress conditions which traps the particles and allows the induced energy to escape as long-wave radiation. There's nothing to worry about unless you actually touch the crystals or get too close.'

'Just like an ordinary fire.' Mathias shook his head and stared up and around the cavern. 'What do you think of it, Alan?'

Carter was standing at a large table on which stood platters heaped with a variety of food. He picked up a portion of roasted lion, smelt it and grinned.

'Meat! Real, honest to God meat! It's worth moving down here just to get away from those yeast and algae surrogates.' He lifted the joint. 'Here's to good food!'

'Don't!' Koenig walked quickly towards the pilot as he lifted the meat to his mouth. 'You can't eat it, Alan. Your metabolism won't accept the local food until you've been adapted.'

'Then let's get adapted.' Reluctantly Carter put down the roasted portion of lion. 'Good food, warmth, a place in which to live and work, extended life—what are we waiting for? When do we evacuate, Commander?'

The question others would be asking as they counted the hours, conscious of the critical period, the shortening time in which to complete exodus.

Koenig looked around the cavern. Helena and Bergman were with Rowland, Frieda and a cluster of others. Tanner weaved among the Thulians, whispering, grimacing, acting the fool with his own purpose. Some who listened to him laughed, others frowned, a few turned away from him, too impatient to pay attention to his babbling.

'Commander?'

Carter was waiting for an answer and Koenig realized that his question had been serious.

He said, 'It's not as simple as that, Alan. There are quite a few here who would rather move to Alpha than spend their lives on Ultima Thule.'

'They must be crazy.' Carter shrugged, casually indifferent to local problems. 'In any case they can't affect us. Let them go to Alpha if they want to. They're welcome to it. We'll take over down here.'

For him it was decided—for others too, Bergman among them.

'John, do you realize that we may be on the threshold of a new step in the evolution of Man? Thulians and Alphans may be the forerunners of a new race of humans which will be as different from ourselves as we are from our remote ancestors.'

'Or maybe we could be stepping into a blind alley,' said Koenig. 'The extended treatment brings sterility, don't forget.'

'A problem which Doctor Rowland is certain we can overcome given time.'

'Even so, it requires consideration.'

'Why, Commander?' Carter frowned. 'What have you got against it?'

'Can't you guess?' Rowland's voice was loud, rising above the hum of conversation to echo from the crystals studding the roof and give rise to sympathetic vibrations which quivered the air like the hum of plucked strings. 'On Alpha John Koenig is the commander and supreme head. A dictator who holds absolute authority over those in his little world. Naturally he is reluctant to yield his power. Once on Ultima Thule every man and woman now under his command will be free to do exactly as they please. He has no desire to see the base evacuated.'

Helena said, flatly, 'I don't believe that is true. In fact I know that it isn't. I am surprised that you should even think it, Doctor Rowland.'

'You, obviously, know the commander better than I, Doctor Russell, and if I have made a false accusation I apologize.'

Yet the damage had been done as Koenig knew, the seed of doubt planted in receptive minds. Those present were loyal, but even Carter was frowning, unable to understand the reluctance to evacuate, and the Thulians would be quick to accept Rowland's explanation.

Koenig said, 'You are asking me to make a serious decision which will affect the lives of others. I need time to make it. Once the thing is decided it cannot be reversed.'

'Because Alpha is passing this world,' said Rowland. 'I understand, Commander, at least I understand the logistics of the situation, but I cannot follow your line of reasoning as to why you should make the decision. I should have thought this was a matter for individual choice. All of you could come here if you wish. Those of you who prefer an early death and the remote chance of bumping into a pleasant planet can stay on Alpha.'

'That sounds reasonable to me, John,' said Helena.

'A democratic choice.' Bergman nodded. Neither he nor the woman had thought the thing through and Carter was equally blind.

'That sounds fair enough to me, Commander. Give everyone a free, individual choice.'

'No,' said Koenig. 'I can't.' Quickly he explained. 'Alpha cannot function without the trained people to operate the base so individual freedom of choice is out of the question. What would we do without our doctors? Our atomic engineers? Our chemists? We must act as a unit in order to survive. Evacuation must be total or not at all. I'm not prepared to make the decision. It must be left to the vote and the majority will decide.'

'But your people must be given all the facts,' said Rowland sharply. 'They must be told what living on Thule will mean to them. I must tell them about our way of life, the hopes we have, the golden promise of a wonderful future which will be theirs once they join us. You will permit me to visit them?'

'Of course.'

'The Alphans have the right to hear another point of view,' said Frieda. 'There's a snake in this paradise and they must be warned about it. Jack, you're our man! You'll speak for us!'

'No!' Tanner spun, gibbering, his eyes glaring, hands lifted to twitch beside his ears. 'I shan't go and neither should you, Cabot. You claim to have destroyed the realm of death, but by all the dishevelled wandering stars I swear to you—death *has* dominion!'

'I'll put the case,' said Koenig. 'Now let's get to the Eagle and on with the job!'

The wind was bad, the static almost solid with electronic noise, but Carter lifted the ship with deft hands.

'We'll have to design atmospheric filters,' he said cheerfully. 'Use the ultra-violet part of the spectrum and key down so as to get a direct visual image. Or we could adapt a sonic scanner to do the job. Ted Foster might think of something, he's one smart engineer.'

'He's had a long time in which to learn,' said Koenig dryly.

'Centuries.' Carter stretched in the pilot's seat and thought about it. 'It seems hard to plan so far ahead. You could start a project now and think of it being finished in a couple of hundred years or so. You know, Commander, once when I was a boy I wanted to grow some trees. We only had a scrap of garden and it was pretty bare and so I wanted to grow trees. Then they told me how long it would take to grow an oak I could climb—hell, I would be old before I could enjoy it. Now that wouldn't apply. A few dozen years, a few decades, what does it matter?'

Koenig said nothing, leaning forward instead to check the instruments.

'Sandra's going to like it on Thule,' continued Carter. 'We'll find a nice, snug little cave and I'll get some fire-crystals and we'll set up a real nice home. It'll be good to go walking for as long as you want without having to worry about air and all that. And we can build—'

'For what, Alan?'

'For the future.' Carter echoed his surprise. 'What else, Commander?'

'A future without children,' said Koenig quietly. 'That's what it means, despite Rowland's promises. Once you adapt to Thule you'll be sterile. That's what Frieda was talking about. She doesn't want us to leave Alpha.'

Carter shrugged. 'She's in no position to talk. She doesn't know what life is like on the Moon.'

'But she knows what it's like on Ultima Thule. That's why she—!' Koenig broke off as Helena screamed from where she sat in the passenger compartment. 'What the hell's that?'

She was sitting, face strained, eyes incredulous, one hand extended, the fingers filled with skeletal bone filmed with slime. More bone as fragile as sun-bleached straw lay on the floor among a litter of furs.

'John! It was—' Helena's voice rose to hover on the edge of hysteria. 'God! Horrible!'

'Steady!' His voice was as effective as a slap across the cheek. 'What happened?'

'I—I touched him, John! I touched him!'

'Victor?'

'It was Rowland,' said Bergman. He sat facing Helena and looked physically ill. 'I saw it happen. We were talking and he had caught hold of Helena's hand and then, suddenly, he simply dissolved.'

Nine centuries of age catching up all at once. An adapted metabolism collapsing as it left the aura-field of the planet. Life forced to take an alien path breaking down as it moved from the only world on which it could survive.

The hidden snake in Rowland's lost paradise.

The Alphans had yet to find a home.